Ring of Lies

Rachel Lynne

We must have perseverance and, above all,
confidence in ourselves ...
Marie Curie

Contents

On Top of The World

Ivy

"Roll upppp ...," I danced between the tables pushing a service cart of supplies. Music blared from the overhead speakers, filling my little café with melodic harmonies. I polished a neon orange surface and then centered a battery-operated lava lamp and salt and pepper shakers while singing along at the top of my lungs. I scooted to the next table. "Waiting to take you away – "

"They need to take you away." My assistant manager and best friend, Tina, yelled as she put away supplies behind the bar. A sharp rap made both of us turn toward the door. Tina smirked and pointed. "See? They're already here." She winked and went into the kitchen.

"Oh, very funny." I laughed and skipped to the door. Nothing was going to dampen my spirits today. I was riding high. Capital, courtesy of my godfather, was in the bank. Supplies were arriving daily, and advertising was well underway.

I flipped the lock on the door. Apparently, the radio spots and flyers were working. Propping the door open with my hip, I smiled as I shook my head. "Sorry guys, we won't be open for another week but y'all are welcome to drop by for the grand opening."

I started to pull the door closed when the younger of the two halted me by wrapping his hand around the door frame.

My eyes widened as I looked the two over. The one holding the door looked to be fresh out of college, while his companion wore a world-weary look that said he'd seen the other side of forty for some time.

Both were dressed in similar, yet unremarkable, navy suits and tan trench coats. An unusual relationship to be sure but who was I to judge? Still, I hadn't thought they'd give me trouble. I gulped, tightened my grip on the door, and flashed a tight smile. "Hey! Come by Friday after next at five p.m. We'll have free samples, live music, it'll be – "

"Ma'am ..." The younger man interrupted. His tone was flat, and his eyes showed nothing but determination. A chill of foreboding ran up my spine.

The older gentleman stepped forward and flashed his badge. "I'm Detective Hallowell with the Savannah PD. This is my partner, Detective Adkins. Mind if we come in?"

My euphoric cloud burst. I opened the door wide and motioned for the detectives to enter, before swallowing past a lump in my throat and shouting for Tina to cut the music.

The music died, leaving an uneasy silence. "Hey! What gives?" Tina's face appeared in the pass-through window. "I thought you said the music kept you movin' and gave the joint good vibes ..." Her gaze flickered over the men before coming to rest on me. "Uh, everything all right?"

I nodded and forced myself to smile. I didn't know why the detectives were here, but it couldn't be good. "These men are with the SPD."

Tina's eyebrows rose and she shot me a questioning look. "Want me to join you?"

I shook my head. Until I knew their purpose wasn't in any way detrimental to my café, it was better not to involve Tina. My friend couldn't keep her mouth shut to save her soul.

I stifled a groan as Detective Adkins decided for me. "If you would, ma'am? We just have a few questions."

Tina was through the swinging door like a shot. She hurried across the room and plopped down onto one of the shiny black wooden chairs. Her face was alight with curiosity as she looked up at them. "So, what's up?"

I rolled my eyes and flashed an apologetic smile. "How can we help you, detectives?"

Detective Hallowell reached into his coat pocket and withdrew a plastic evidence bag. Condensation beaded the surface and made the contents appear fuzzy, but I would have recognized the tie-dye patterned paper even before he turned it over to expose the fat black letters filled with white stars that spelled out Cosmic Café.

The detective held it up in front of me and asked, "This yours?"

I licked my lips and nodded, remaining silent. From years on the road with Aunt Fey, I'd learned never to offer any information not specifically requested.

The detective stared at me for a long minute, not bothering to hide his speculation. He cleared his throat and then slipped the bag back into his pocket. "Thought so. I know these things are all over town but this one has the name Ivy scrawled on the bottom with an address on Gwinnett."

I sucked in a breath. "My ... my name is Ivy and I live on Gwinnett." My stomach churned. Someone involved in a crime had my name and address. I swallowed hard and forced my voice not to tremble. "What is going on?"

Detective Hallowell held his hand out toward his partner. "We pulled a body out of the river this morning. She had this flyer in her pocket." Without warning, he thrust a picture under my nose. "Do you recognize this woman?"

I gasped and sank into a chair. I raised a shaking hand to my mouth and stared at the photo. My breath came in short pants and pinpoints of light filled my eyes. I opened my mouth, but no sound came out.

"Ivy!" Tina leaped from her chair and tried to push my head between my knees. "Breathe girl, breathe!" Tina slapped the photo away from my face. "For God's sake man, put that away!"

"Ma'am, I'm sorry to distress you but I need to know who this woman is."

"Leave her alone! It's obvious she knows the poor woman- "

"No ..., no, Tina, it's all right." I pulled away from Tina and dragged a shaking hand through my hair. "I, I know who she ..." My voice broke on a sob and tears spilled down my cheeks unheeded.

I wrapped my arms around my midsection and rocked in the chair as the truth sank in. It couldn't be true; she didn't even live in Savannah.

"Ma'am?" Detective Hallowell prodded.

I looked at the detectives and struggled to rein in my emotions long enough to whisper, "That ..., that's my Aunt Fey."

A Heavy Heart

Ivy

I scrunched up my nose and fought the urge to gag. The smell of sweat, empty pizza boxes, and greasy chicken buckets permeated the sorry excuse of a room. I kicked at a pile of dirty clothes and grimaced as a family of roaches scurried away to hide under a pile of newspapers.

"Oh, gross!" Tina muttered. She pursed her mouth and picked up an open coke can with two fingers, setting it beside the overflowing trashcan. She turned, hands on her hips, and demanded, "Ivy, do we seriously have to go through this stuff?"

I sighed and looked around the run-down, rent-by-the-week efficiency apartment that had been Aunt Fey's last known address. I didn't blame my friend for being disgusted. Putting aside the rank smells, if one could manage it, the place was a wreck.

Half-opened dresser drawers spilled their contents onto the stained red carpet. Paperback thrillers with torn covers and dog-eared pages lay in a jumbled heap next to an overturned sofa that had seen better days.

Empty coke cans and crumpled candy wrappers, strewn across the coffee table's sticky surface, attested to Fey's recent presence. I righted a ladder-back kitchen chair and then thought better of sitting; every surface in the sad little room was grimy.

I gave Tina a halfhearted smile. "You don't have to stay. I can do this." I waved a hand toward the jumbled mess.

Tina gave me a dirty look. "Like I'd leave you to go through this junk alone. What kind of a friend do you think I am?"

I smiled. "The best kind." I dropped the empty boxes we'd brought from the café. "Honestly, I doubt there is much I'll keep. Aunt Fey believed in traveling light and not being weighed down by material things so I'm guessing there isn't much here. I think I'll load the bulk of this stuff up and drop it at the mission charity shop. What do you think?"

Tina's face screwed into a look of disgust as she picked up an empty pizza box and a grease-stained paper plate. "What do I think? I think we should light a match."

I cocked my head and raised an eyebrow in response to the flippant remark.

"Oh, all right, we'll go through this junk. Pack up what you want, and take off." Tina moved towards a pile of clothing. "Oh, and be sure to fumigate everything with roach spray before you unload it at your place!"

I laughed. "Yeah, sounds like a plan." I looked around and tried to decide what area might hold something of even sentimental value. My relationship with my guardian had been a rocky one, and even though we hadn't spoken in four years, I still wanted something tangible to mark Fey's existence in the world.

The lack of anything belonging to my parents had been a bone of contention between us since my teens. Our last fight was, in part, over that very thing.

I sighed as my mind drifted back to the one-room cabin nestled in the Shenandoah Valley. A fire roared in the old potbellied stove, making the sparsely furnished space a cozy place to ride out the snowstorm rattling the windows. The atmosphere inside was anything but cozy, though. Fey and I were at each other's throats, again.

I threw my hands up in disgust. "All I want to know is why. Why can't I go back to Georgia and use my parents' insurance money to go to college?"

Fey sighed, set down her beading needle, and removed her magnifying glasses. She pinched the bridge of her nose and pushed the half-finished Egyptian-styled bracelet aside before meeting my eyes. "Ivy, you're acting like a hormone-filled teenager."

I rolled my eyes. "I am a teenager!" I'm seventeen or have you forgotten?"

"No, I haven't forgotten you are a teenager." She averted her eyes and mumbled, "Seventeen? Hmm."

I let out an exasperated huff. "Aunt Fey, I turned seventeen nine months ago, during your pottery phase, remember?"

Fey's eyes widened as light dawned. "Oh yeah, I remember now. We'd just arrived from Oregon." She smiled and looked around the neat little room. "Can't believe we've been a part of the artist colony for so long ... seems like only yesterday-"

"We are not part of Maidenwood; you are a part of it. I'm just the kid who fetches clay for the sculptors, ferries pottery to the kiln, and stretches canvas for the "would-be artists.""

"Well, you are an apprentice. You get to experience the various vocations while you find your chosen medium." She looked down her nose at me. "It is an experience many people would love to have, dear. You should be more appreciative. They don't let just anyone live and work here, you know, and they certainly don't make apprentices out of high school kids."

"Aunt Fey!" I stamped my foot. "I am not in high school. I graduated early just before we left Oregon-with honors I might add."

Fey's brow wrinkled. "Don't be silly; of course, you're still in school ...' she bit her lip. "Why you've just started your junior year; I'm sure of it."

She graced me with a beaming smile and began to thread a length of red and gold beads onto her needle, the issue closed in her mind.

I thought the top of my head would explore. Fey could be incredibly obtuse when it suited her purposes. I bit back a smart-ass retort; sarcasm was lost on my aunt. "Look Aunt Fey, I know what an honor it is to be invited to live and work here. It's a testament to natural talent that they invited you even though you've never had a show or formal training or ... or anything. But, you see, I don't have any artistic ability and I'm not remotely interested in being an artist. I want – "

"Ivy don't put yourself down! You are an artist in the kitchen ... why everyone says so."

I saw red. "Aunt Fey! That is what I'm trying – "I stopped and drew a deep breath. Composure was need-ed to argue with Fey. "Thank you for the compliment but that is what I've been saying. I want to use the rest of Mom and Dad's life insurance money to attend culinary school. I don't see why- "

"But why must you go to school in Atlanta? There is a perfectly good school in D.C., I've checked."

My eyes narrowed. Aunt Fey's question proved she was neither oblivious nor uninterested. "Why not Atlanta? Georgia is home and I want to go back."

My aunt concentrated on her beading, refusing to meet my eyes or acknowledge I was speaking. My face flushed as anger surged through me. It was time to take a stand. I gritted my teeth and then stomped my foot. "I'm going to school in Atlanta and, as soon as I've graduated, I'm moving back to Savannah, whether you like it or not!"

I sniffed and swiped at the moisture welling in my eyes. That day seemed so long ago, a lifetime really, and the result had been the breakdown of my relationship with Aunt Fey. My decision to return to Savannah had shocked her to the core and caused a riff that I was powerless to mend. After numerous attempts, I'd given up, telling myself that time would heal the wound; but time, for Aunt Fey, had run out.

I shook my head and tried to concentrate on the jumbled mess surrounding me, but the tears continued to flow.

"Ivy? You all right?"

Embarrassed, I nodded and quickly turned away from Tina. I searched the room for a box of tissues and spotted a pile of crumpled take-out napkins on the breakfast bar. They'd have to do.

I blew my nose and then jumped as a hand fell onto my shoulder. I turned and flinched at the sympathy I saw reflected in my friends' eyes. The last thing I wanted to do was break down in front of someone, even Tina.

I was the strong one, the one who had it all together, the one everyone else turned to for advice and support; I never lost it. I stiffened my shoulders and nodded. "Yeah." I cleared my throat and tried to laugh. "Yeah, I'm fine, Tina. I must have gotten something in my- "

"Don't bullshit me, Ivy; we've been friends too long."

"I'm not ..." My shoulders drooped, and fresh tears formed. "You're right; I'm not fine."

Tina smiled and wrapped her arms around me. "Want to talk about it?"

I shook my head and broke free of Tina's embrace. I scrubbed at the moisture continuing to fall down my cheeks. "God! This is so stupid!" I rolled my eyes and reached for more napkins. "I don't know what's the matter with me."

"Girl! Quit being so hard on yourself. Your only living relative, the lady who raised you, is dead, murdered for God's sake; I'd think you were strange if you didn't cry!"

I chuckled and blew my nose again. "You're right. I thought I was dealing with it but looking at Fey's stuff ... well, it just hit me hard. I am finally facing the fact that she is gone and I ... we didn't part on the best of terms." I nudged a pile of yellowed newspapers closer to the trash can with the toe of my shoe and fought back more tears.

"You never did say why you two weren't speaking ..."

I drew a shaky breath. "She was mad that I wanted to come back to Savannah. I don't know why but the idea of coming home made her mad- no, that's not right. Aunt Fey wasn't mad; it was more like she was afraid."

Tina frowned. "Why would she be afraid?"

I shrugged. "I don't know, and she never would tell me. I just know what I saw on her face the last time we spoke. I'd just graduated from culinary school, and I told her I was moving to Savannah; I asked her to move with me. I had this plan to open a café someday, ya know?"

Tina grinned. "And you did!"

I sniffed and smiled. "Yeah, yeah, I, well we did! But at the time, I had thought it would be cool to open a café combined with an art gallery or something, but Aunt Fey freaked at the suggestion. It was obvious she was terrified of the idea but when I tried to talk to her about it, she shut down."

I ran a hand through my hair and sighed. "She was disappointed when I chose to go to school in Atlanta, but we still talked on the phone, and I returned to Virginia during school breaks. But when I moved here, that just wrecked everything. She stopped taking my calls and I ... I guess I was mad because she was being so stubborn. I sent cards at Christmas and her birthday, but I refused to visit."

I fought back a fresh wave of tears.

Tina wrapped an arm around my waist and squeezed gently. "Don't blame yourself, Ivy. It sounds like you made an effort to mend things. The ball was in your aunt's court."

I swallowed hard. "I know, but I should have pushed the issue. I should have forced her to explain or ..." I turned my head and met Tina's gaze. "I ... I guess I just thought there'd be plenty of time ..."

Tina nodded. "Everybody does, Ivy; it's human nature." Tina's lips twitched into a ghost of a smile. "You have to accept that some things are out of your control. You can't make people do what they don't want to, Ms. Fix-it."

My lips curled into a rueful smile. My friends were always teasing me about my managing tendencies. I drew a deep breath and forcefully exhaled. Tina was right. I'd tried to repair the relationship with Fey; the rest had been up to her. "You're right. It's hard to accept but the truth is, Aunt Fey wasn't willing to meet me halfway. It hurts but ..."

I gave Tina a quick hug and then stepped back, straightening my shoulders. "Time to push aside the past and get to work. Thanks for letting me unload on you."

Tina grinned. "Anytime Ivy, what are friends for? God only knows how many times I've cried on your shoulder."

I grinned and ticked off a list with my fingers. "Well, there was the time you caught that famous-in-his-own-mind chef in the walk-in cooler with the pastry chef ... and let's not forget that fiasco with the movie stuntman- "

Tina rolled her eyes. "Geesh! I'm well aware of my rocky love life; no need to rub it in!"

I widened my eyes and tried to look innocent. "You're the one who brought it up; I'm just helping you keep count." I held up another finger. "You never fully explained what set you off the night I had to drag you from the No Quarter, but since you were wasted and shouting your phone number at the bartender when I arrived, I have always assumed he lied when he said he'd call."

I laughed and ignored Tina's rude hand gesture. "I also remember all too well how heartbroken you were when it didn't work out with the wannabe rock star."

I regretted the words as soon as they left my mouth. Sadness replaced the twinkle in Tina's eyes, and I noticed her lower lip tremble before she turned away. "Oh God, I'm sorry, Tina! I shouldn't have mentioned that ..."

Tina sniffed and waved a dismissive hand in my direction. "S'okay, Ivy. What happened with Ian ... well ..." she shrugged then turned to meet my eyes. "I've moved on. It was a long time ago and hey, there are other fish in the sea, right?"

I nodded but held my tongue. Tina might lie to herself, but I knew better. The end of Tina's relationship with Ian Buchanan haunted my friend. Several times in recent years, a drunk and rambling Tina had filled my ears with her grief over the musician who'd dumped her before leaving Savannah in pursuit of stardom; it didn't help that he was succeeding.

When sober, Tina never talked about Ian and I always followed her lead, until now. I bit my lip and searched for something to say.

Tina cleared her throat. "Hey! We gonna start packing or just stand here soaking up this four-star ambiance?"

I laughed, grateful for the change in subject. Wallowing in regret served no purpose, for me or Tina. A smile curved my lips as I remembered one of Aunt Fey's oft-repeated sayings. The past is littered with holes of regrets so don't retrace your steps or you might fall in.

I pushed the lingering sadness to the back of my mind and surveyed the room. The place was a disaster. "Hmmm, what would you call this place? Upscale wino?"

Tina snorted and put her hands on her hips. "The word upscale in no way applies to this joint." She shook her head. "Where do you want me to start?"

"Umm, do you mind packing up those books?"

Tina wrinkled her nose. "Ok, but I'd rather clean this place up. This mess is driving me nuts, not to mention the outright filth ... it reeks!"

"I know, but don't bother. I'm going to take what I want, throw out the junk, and leave. The management can clean; it's their dump."

I grabbed a box and headed toward a battered dresser sitting opposite the upended sofa. The small, clean square on its surface suggested a television had once occupied the spot. I briefly wondered if someone had helped themselves to the set or if Aunt Fey had pawned it; either option was a distinct possibility.

Tina snorted and picked a lamp up off the floor. She set it onto the dresser and then bent to begin packing the books. "Ok, but no offense? I kinda think this mess was your aunt's. I mean, who rents a place with furniture turned over and garbage spread across the floor?"

I shrugged and tossed an armful of clothes into the charity box. "Aunt Fey wasn't a neat freak like you, but she never lived like this, at least not when I was with her." I closed the last dresser drawer and looked around for another place to begin working. I spotted a drawer underneath the breakfast bar. "This place looks like someone searched it, ya know? I guess, when she didn't come back for a couple of days, the neighbors decided to help themselves."

Tina laughed and dropped an armful of books into the box. "Who'd want this junk? Unless they took the good stuff?"

I shook my head and pulled a wire-bound notebook from the drawer. It was an artist's sketchpad. I flipped through it, smiling at Aunt Fey's drawings of the river, local folks, and the various squares. The price sticker showed it was from an area art store which made me wonder just how long my aunt had been in town. Better question, why?

I turned another page and gasped. I was staring at myself. Fey had caught me outside, washing the windows of the café.

I had signed the lease at the end of December and taken possession a week later, so Fey had been in Savannah for at least three weeks. I thumbed through the rest of the filled pages and found several more portraits- one of me and Tina laying on a blanket in Forsyth Park while my cat batted at his stuffed mouse on a string toy, and another as I planted pansies along the courtyard fence.

I fought back tears and set the book in my box of things to keep. Fey had been watching me for weeks, yet she had never made contact. My lip trembled. Aunt Fey could conquer her fear of Savannah but not muster up forgiveness for her niece.

A grunt from Tina drew my attention. I pushed thoughts of my aunt aside and turned to see my friend struggling to set the battered couch back on its feet. I shook my head and grinned. "What are you doing?"

"I'm sorry but I can't stand it. This mess is driving me crazy. You know how obsessive I am. Come over here and help!"

I laughed. "All right, but I don't know why you're bothering. I know you. You won't be able to stop at putting the furniture back, you'll have to dust, wash dishes, even straighten the pictures!"

I stooped and grabbed my end. "On three. One, two ... there, happy now?" I wiped my hands on my jeans and started back across the room, determined to check the kitchen, and then head out the door. There was surely nothing else worth keeping.

"I'm not washing those dishes; they have fuzz on them!" Tina hollered. "And the table might fall apart without its layer of dust."

I laughed and opened a couple of cabinets, watching more roaches scurry. I shuddered and backed away; nothing could be worth looking any further. I returned to the living room and grabbed the box of clothes, walking towards the door. "I'm finished; you ready to go?"

Tina deposited an armful of magazines on top of her box of books. "And how!" She cast a final glance around her area and grinned. "Just let me straighten this fabulous, and obviously lost work of a master to assuage my sense of order and we'll go."

I laughed. "Tina, for goodness's sake, let it go, fight the urge – "

"Hey, what's this?" Tina frowned and peeked behind the picture.

I set my box down and joined Tina at the wall behind the sofa. "What's what? Whatever it is can't be gross, or you'd be screaming." I stopped as Tina held out a small silver key.

She handed it to me.

"My fingers brushed it when I grabbed the frame. It was taped to the back. Do you think it belonged to your aunt?"

I turned the key over in my hand. It looked like a safety deposit box key but what could Aunt Fey have owned that needed to be stored so securely? I read the worn engraving- Islands Bank and Trust.

Memories of the day we'd left Savannah crashed in on me. I was nine years old, and Aunt Fey stood in the doorway of my bedroom flipping the lights on and off. I groaned and asked what was going on. She answered that we were going to find a change of scenery. I was to pack light and be ready in ten minutes.

"Earth to Ivy."

I jumped and shook off the cobwebs of the past. "I'm sorry; I was lost in thought."

"Obviously. You were a million miles away. So, do I take it the key belonged to your aunt?"

I nodded. "Yeah, I think it does. I remember Aunt Fey putting a key like that into her pocket the day we left Savannah."

Tina raised her eyebrows, skepticism written on her face. "I'm not sayin' the key isn't your aunt's, but you were like what, ten when you left? Why would you remember such a small thing?"

I stared at the key as a vivid picture of that pivotal moment rose in my mind. "I was nine," I absently corrected Tina, "but I remember the day clearly. Mom and Dad had just died, and Aunt Fey was staying at the house with me. That morning she woke me and said we were leaving. I shoved some stuff into a backpack and climbed into the car. We stopped in front of this big old house in the historic district. Aunt Fey made me stay in the car, but I read the sign on the gate; it was a law office. She wouldn't tell me why we were there, but she came back to the car with a thick envelope. After that, we stopped at the bank."

"You think the key opens a safety deposit box?"

I nodded. "Yeah, at the time, I didn't know that's what she'd done, but looking back it makes perfect sense.

There weren't any close parking spots so I couldn't be left in the car. Aunt Fey grabbed the envelope and a box lying on the back seat and then we walked to the bank. I sat in the lobby while she went with a bank employee. She came back empty-handed, except for a little silver key. I asked her where the box was, but she ignored me. She slipped the key into her pocket, grabbed my hand, and raced to the car. A few minutes later, we were on the train heading to Jacksonville."

"Huh. She never told you why she went to the bank?"

I shook my head "Nope. It was very hard to get Aunt Fey to talk about the past. I was seventeen before I learned she'd sold my parents' house. The money from the house and their life insurance policy was what I used to pay my college tuition and partially start the Cosmic."

Tina shoved her box of books closer to the door. "From what you've told me about your childhood, I'm surprised there was any money left."

I smiled and followed Tina to the door. "As flighty as she could be with most things, Aunt Fey felt very strongly about my inheritance. She took only enough for necessities and then only when she couldn't find any other way to provide for us."

Tina grinned. "The way you tell it, your aunt was pretty creative in her way of supporting you guys!"

I smirked. Aunt Fey's way of making ends meet had led to an interesting if unusual life. I had grown tired of the constant moving and Aunt Fey's ever-changing boyfriends. I'd made up my mind to live a different life when I'd settled on going to culinary school. I wanted to live in one place, have a routine, and make friends; in short, I wanted an uneventful, normal life.

A sense of dread crept over me as I looked at the key. Average people, living average lives, kept innocuous things in bank boxes but Fey had been anything but average. There was no telling what was stashed at the bank.

I sighed and slipped the key into my pocket; so much for my plan to live a boring life. I picked up my box and motioned for Tina to follow. "Let's go before the stench in here is permanently etched into my nose."

Tina laughed and trotted down the stairs as I pulled the door closed. "You want to stay here while I get the car?"

I shook my head and hefted the box higher onto my hip. "Nah, not unless you think yours is too heavy. This one is nothing but clothes and a sketchpad."

Tina shrugged and headed for the sidewalk. "Mine is full of paperbacks, I can manage. I'm just glad to be out of there; what a depressing place!"

I nodded absently. Unlike Tina, I was aware that we weren't in the best of neighborhoods. I was on high alert. I didn't say anything because Tina was forever telling me I was paranoid, but I'd spotted a guy sitting in his car not far from where we were parked. We'd walk right by him in another minute.

He was huge, his head brushed the car's ceiling, and he took up most of the front seat. I wouldn't want to tangle with him. I took a deep breath and tensed as we closed in on the car. Another couple of steps and we'd be next to the driver's door ...I told myself to get a grip and tried to focus on what Tina was saying.

"I can't wait to hear what your Aunt Fey put in that safety deposit box. I'm assuming you remember which bank she took you to all those years ago?"

I nodded and tried not to make eye contact with the man in the car. "Yeah, but even if I didn't, Islands Bank is engraved on the key."

Tina's eyes widened. "Hey! What if old Fey stashed a bunch of money in it?"

I laughed, feeling better now that we'd passed the man's car. "You have a vivid imagination. I don't know what Fey put in the bank box, but I'm guessing it's not money. Probably birth certificates and stuff."

Tina huffed and pushed the button on her car keys, unlocking the car. "You take all my fun away." She popped the trunk, and we secured our boxes before sliding into the car.

I smirked and fastened my seatbelt. "You'll live."

Tina stuck her tongue out before cranking the car and pulling away from the curb. "I choose to believe there is something exciting awaiting you. Maybe it's a map to hidden treasure or a sack full of rare coins ..." she waved a hand dismissively. "Whatever ..., I refuse to believe it is anything as boring as legal records."

I rolled my eyes and cranked up the radio, positive my friend had a loose screw. Though I had to admit, with offbeat Aunt Fey, none of the things Tina had listed was beyond the realm of possibility: Trouble was, one never knew just what Fey considered treasures.

Pandora's Box

Ivy

I stood outside Islands Bank and Trust and tried to calm my fluttering stomach. I bit my lip and wiped my sweaty palms down the sides of my skirt, a second before remembering I was wearing my best silk wrap. "Crap! I hope I didn't mark it."

I rolled my eyes and acknowledged I was being ridiculous and irrational. All through the long weekend, I'd fretted over the little silver key, wondering and worrying until I'd gotten a sick headache.

It hadn't helped that Tina continued to insist the bank box must contain something valuable. Her argument being why else would Fey have hidden the key?

I couldn't explain my aunt's behavior any more than I could explain my unease; honestly, it was more like dread. The story of Pandora's Box kept crossing my mind, mixing with my inexplicable feeling that whatever the contents of the box, the lid should remain closed, lest secrets be revealed.

The sad truth was, that Aunt Fey had lived life in a whirlwind of emotion and excitement. She changed men like other people changed toothbrushes. Until she'd found herself at the artists' colony, Aunt Fey had lived off of men, and, when one wasn't available, she was scheming- anything to make a buck.

That knowledge was at the heart of my hesitation; the adage about sleeping dogs and all that. But I'd come anyway. Tina's prodding, I could have ignored but, I had made the mistake of discussing everything with James Brogan. It'd been my godfather who convinced me to not leave loose ends.

I was dubious of his assertion that knowing was better than wondering but he was so insistent that I check the bank box's contents and it was hard not to give in since it was his silent partnership loan that had allowed me to start the Cosmic Café years earlier than my business plan projections forecasted.

So, I'd pushed myself out the door and walked the five blocks to Johnson Square, enjoying the unusually warm February day, while trying to find any excuse to delay my arrival, but none presented itself. Now I had to muster the courage to go inside and face whatever awaited me.

I squared my shoulders and told myself that all the trepidation was nonsense, and it was time to get a move on; giving the tinted glass door a shove, I strode inside.

Ivy

I clutched the large manila envelope to my chest and waved my thanks to the assistant manager as I walked past his cubicle. I shook my head and laughed at my earlier fears. All that build-up for what amounted to little more than a bundle of legal papers and some crumpled receipts. I grinned. It felt good to finally know where all of my parents' things were stored.

I'd also found a stack of old photos that I couldn't wait to look through, some yellowed newspaper clippings, and, at the bottom of the metal drawer, buried beneath the loose papers, I'd found a tangled mess of tarnished silver chains, a couple of rings, and a pocket watch that I vaguely recalled being my grandfather's.

Far from unearthing Aunt Fey's dark secrets, I'd caught a glimpse of her sentimental side, if the old photos and jewelry were any indication. I had lost count of the number of times I'd bugged Fey for stories or pictures of our family. Her response was always the same. "Whatcha want to go livin' in the past for? Ya gotta live in the now, Ivy girl, leave the past where it belongs; in the ground."

No matter how much I argued, Fey could never grasp my desire to know more about my ancestry, and I struggled to explain it. I just knew I wanted a connection to the family I'd lost a week after my ninth birthday; I wanted to know where I came from. I longed for roots and a permanent home surrounded by people and things that told the story of my life. Fey asserted that holding on to material things weighed down the spirit, but I wanted that anchor.

The aroma of freshly brewed coffee drew me like a magnet as I crossed Broughton Street. I spared a guilty glance at the blinking light on my phone and then entered the crowded coffee shop.

Ten minutes and two more voice mails later, I managed to snag a seat outside, overlooking the busy street. I took a cautious sip of skinny vanilla latte then sighed and checked my phone.

Several vendors calls, that were better dealt with in my office, and ten showed that Tina was dying of curiosity. Two more from my godfather suggested he wasn't much better off. I took pity and pushed speed dial, laughing as Tina answered on the first ring.

"Good grief," I teased, "are you getting any work done?"

"I'll have you know I put away all of the new dishes, took inventory of the things we still need and am now keeping your godfather company, so there!"

"Jamie is there?" My eyes widened. "Well, glad to hear you managed to accomplish something in between phone calls."

"Oh, funny, haha. I didn't call that many times – "

"Girl! There are ten voice mails on- "

"Hold on, Ivy, Mr. Brogan wants to talk to you."

"Ivy? You there?"

I shook my head, amazed that he was so impatient. "Yes Jamie, I'm here, but I'll be back at the café in about ten minutes."

"Can't wait any longer, Darlin;' I have a meeting. I just wanted to see if you were all right, and you weren't answering your phone. Hang up and I'll call you back once I'm in the car."

I rolled my eyes but did as he'd commanded. Less than a minute later, the caller ID showed my godfather's name. "Hi Jamie, I wish you could wait, I'd fix you lunch."

"That sounds wonderful, but this meeting can't wait. So, tell me ... was opening the box as bad as you expected?"

I laughed and set off towards the café. "You were right. I was being silly. Aunt Fey had all kinds of great stuff in there."

"Really? Like what?"

"Oh, nothing you'd be interested in. Just family stuff. So, what brought you to the Cosmic- "

"What was in the box, Ivy?"

I stopped in the middle of the sidewalk, shocked at his tone and abrupt interruption. *What the hell?* His casual chatter of a moment ago was gone, replaced with a harsh, almost demanding tone I'd heard from him on occasion, though never with me. I shook off my irritation, telling myself he cared about me and wanted to share in my excitement, but he was a busy, important man.

"Ivy?"

"I'm here. Sorry, I got distracted. What was in the box?" I tossed the cup in a trash can and started across the Square. "Let's see, there were some documents about my parents' estate, a bunch of old receipts, and some yellowed newspaper articles, "

I laughed and shifted the phone to my other ear. "No idea why Fey kept those, one was about an old robbery or something. Anyway, you'll never guess what else was in there!"

"Oh? Why don't you tell me, then?"

I frowned, still getting the feeling my godfather was ... angry, intense? I couldn't define what I was hearing in his voice, but it made me antsy. I shook off my misgivings, he was a busy man, with no time for childish games. "Sorry Jamie, I know you're busy. Aunt Fey kept a stack of old pictures, and you know how much I've wanted to know more about my family."

I waited for a tourist trolley to pass and then jogged across Oglethorpe to beat the traffic. "I just can't believe what she kept! One is of my dad as a kid. He's dressed like a cowboy and sitting on a pony! Another is of him beside a red stingray and I'm guessing the guy next to him is you!"

"Is that right? Well, I remember when he got that car, we used to tear up the roads ..."

I smiled, glad to hear the familiar, jovial tone back in his voice. "I want to hear about that!" I laughed. "So, what do you think about her keeping them? Pretty cool, considering Aunt Fey's philosophy about family and things, huh?"

Jamie snorted and drawled. "That is very *cool*, Darlin'. You know we all like to think we're immune, but the lure of the past is powerful. It pulls you back no matter how far or how fast you run."

I chuckled. "Geez, Jamie. That's pretty cynical, dontcha think?"

"Wait until you get to be my age, girl, then we'll see who is being cynical."

I laughed. "We'll see. So, where are you? I'm walking through the park right now, maybe you could swing by, and we could grab a bite- "

"Sorry, Darlin', Rizzo drives fast. We're halfway across town now. I'm meeting my war party for lunch. The final push of my campaign."

"Oh, I'm sorry I missed you but that is awesome! You'll make a great congressman."

A rich chuckle flowed down the line, and I rolled my eyes at my earlier misgivings; he was the same tried and true best friend of my father's and greatest godfather a girl could ever have that he'd always been.

"Thanks, Darlin'." He paused and when he spoke again the lazy humor was gone, replaced with the same tone I'd noted earlier. "Ivy? Was there anything else in the bank box?"

I frowned and tried to shake my strange thoughts off. What was it I was hearing in his voice? Distraction? Maybe, but there was something ... off. I sighed, it had to be all of the emotions stirred up with the death of Aunt Fey; I was just out of sorts, and then with the café due to open ...

"Ivy! Are you there?"

I jumped. "Huh? Oh yeah, sorry. I was just thinking about how much I have on my mind and how much I have left to do ... "I laughed. "I think I'm going to drop this stuff off at the house before I go to the café. Tina will bug me to death if I bring it in and then nothing will get done, you know?"

"Spoken like a true business owner. I'm proud of you." His voice lowered and I heard him speaking to someone in the background. I frowned as I caught the word net and later; was her debonair godfather taking up fishing? I was just about to tease him when he came back on the line.

Sorry about that, we've arrived. You never did tell me if there was anything else in your aunt's bank box ..."

I blinked. "Didn't I? Um, pictures, newspaper clippings, that's about it ..." I stepped off the curb, crossing to the block housing my townhome. "Oh yeah, there was a mess of old jewelry! One of the pieces was an old pocket watch I believe was my granddad's! I'm going to run it over to Park Jewelers eventually, see if they can get it running." I picked up my mail and trotted up the stairs to the house. "I'm so excited. Hard to believe I was so afraid to open the thing, huh? After I get the Cosmic up and running, I can spend some time investigating, see who all the pics are of and stuff, won't that be great?"

"Yes, yes that will be nice, Ivy. Look, I'm late so let's talk later, hmm?" Muted voices and the clink of dishes and cutlery came through the phone line. "Oh, by the way, will you be working late at the café?"

I wedged the phone to my ear with my shoulder and slipped the key into the lock. "Uhh, yeah, probably ..." I pushed the door open a couple of inches and immediately filled the space with my foot as a fluffy white face with big blue eyes appeared in the crack. Sergeant shoved against my foot and threatened to bite, making me lose my grip on the mail and bank envelope. "Crap! Sergeant stop- "

"Ivy? What's going on?"

I bent over and shoved the indignant Persian cat back into the apartment then picked up the scattered mail. "Nothing, Jamie, just wrestling with the cat. I better go get him some food; it always calms him down."

Jamie laughed. "Go and tame that beast. Don't work too hard and call me before you leave the café. I want to make sure you get home safely."

I straightened and rubbed the small of my back as I glanced at the clock. No wonder it hurt. I'd been unloading boxes for over four hours. Dropping the last bit of cutlery into the drawer, I headed for the cooler. A latte would have hit the spot, but the coffee man wouldn't have everything set up until tomorrow afternoon. I'd have to make do with a can of organic root beer and a handful of Tina's homemade gingersnaps. I snorted. *Some dinner for a chef.*

A gleam of blue light danced on the wall beside me as I popped the top on the soda. I smiled and turned my hand to the fluorescent lights; glad I'd slid the ring onto my finger before I came to work. It was too big and too blue to be anything other than junk jewelry, but it must have meant something to Aunt Fey, why else would she have kept it in the bank? The large, square-cut stone might be worthless blue glass but wearing it made me feel like I was connected to my aunt, and it cheered me up; right now, that was all that mattered.

I propped my feet up on the window ledge and stared out at the park across the street. Twilight was fading fast and now I'd have to walk the three blocks to my townhouse in the dark. I shouldn't have stayed so late. Remembering my godfather's words, I considered calling him, but he'd insist on giving me a ride and I hated to drag him out when he was so busy. I was dialing Tina's number when the phone rang.

"Speak of the devil," I murmured, then frowned as I read the caller ID. Not Tina but my upstairs neighbor. Eyes wide, I mashed the green button. "Hey, Mac, what's up?"

"Ivy! Where are you?" Mac's voice rattled the phone speaker and the panicked tone in his voice set my internal alarm bells ringing.

"I'm at the Cosmic. What's wrong?"

"Girl! You need to get on home. Owen and I just got back from dinner, and we found your door hanging wide open and Sergeant Pepper taking a bath on the stairs!"

"What?" I screeched and leaped from the chair. I ran through the café frantically cutting off lights as I yelled into the phone. "Is Sergeant all right? Don't let him get outside, Mac; you know how he tries to get outside. God! If he gets out, I'll never find him- "

"Calm down, girl, your cat is fine. I told you, he's licking his junk right in the landing for all to see; no shame in that one."

I bit back a scream of frustration as the line went quiet. In the background, I could hear someone laugh and then something about Mac's being 'jealous'. I tapped my foot, hollering for Mac to get back on the phone.

"Hey, sorry girl; Owen's just messing around- "

"Mac! Where is Sergeant? If he gets out "

"Look, don't' worry about the cat; he's fine and I'm gonna risk life and limb and move him to our apartment. You lock up and sit tight. I'm sending Owen over to get you and I'll call the police, okay?"

I sighed and sank into a chair as the adrenaline rush waned. "Okay, I'll be waiting. And Mac? Thank you."

"No problem, doll. See ya in a few."

I stared out the front window as a knot of cold fear settled in my stomach. I'd lived in Savannah for four years and never a hint of a problem. There were bars on the basement windows of the restored townhouse but most of the homes in the historic district had them. Nobody thought much of it these days. They were a holdover from the late seventies and early eighties when the old homes were dilapidated, and some of the neighborhoods were slightly seedy. That had all changed when men like my godfather started buying the old homes, restoring them to their former glory, and encouraging preservation efforts.

Today, Savannah's historic district was a multibillion-dollar tourist draw that still managed to function as the city's business center. Crime wasn't unheard of, but I had been lucky enough not to experience it. My luck had run out.

I sighed and whispered a prayer for mercy, "Please don't' let it be trashed. I have all I can take right now. I don't think my plate can get any fuller."

Out of the Blue

Dom

I leaned against the dayglow yellow wall and grinned. The Cosmic Café certainly lived up to its name; from the deep green concrete floors to the black ceiling glowing with about a million stars ... the place was incredible; much like its owner.

My position in the front corner of the dining room afforded a perfect view of the long-legged beauty the assistant manager had said was the owner. With a view like that, I didn't mind being kept waiting.

I couldn't pinpoint what it was about her that kept drawing my eye. Maybe it was her legs, which were a mile long. She stepped aside for a delivery guy to pass, and my eyebrows rose. The tie-dyed t-shirt with a peace sign logo proved she was consistent with her décor choices, but it also set my teeth on edge.

The new wannabe hippies with their liberal utopian politics and organic food fanaticism drove me crazy. Most of the young college kids in town lived off of Daddy's money and spouted crap.

They didn't know what it was like to live in the real world any more than their parents did; a bunch of morons who never came out of their ivory towers and gated communities long enough to see the havoc their irresponsible and unrealistic policies created. They needed to walk a mile in my shoes, or rather the shoes I'd worn when I still carried a badge.

I smirked. Judging by the girl's taste in clothing and the café's décor, she was a full-fledged, card-carrying member of the party of nuts and that was a shame because my fingers itched to comb through her mass of dark red curls.

To distract myself, I looked down at my clipboard and reviewed the information obtained by my secretary. The paperwork showed a recent break-in, and that the owner was interested in a full security system at two locations. So, the lady wanted security. I was happy to oblige. I snorted. I'd be her bodyguard for free.

No age or birthdate but I'd put her at no more than twenty-seven. Ivy Michaels. It suited her. She gave off the Earth mother vibe. I glanced up and our gazes locked. She held up one slender finger and mouthed, *"sorry"*, before flashing a brilliant smile and turning her attention back to whomever, she was talking to in the kitchen.

The dazzling smile made me gulp and wish for a glass of water, though I wasn't sure if I'd use it to wet my dry mouth or cool my raging hormones. My gaze roamed over her face. She was a knock-out, all creamy skin, and big dark eyes. I wondered what color they were. I squinted but the distance was too great. No matter, with that coloring she had to be Irish, and I'd bet her eyes were blue; deep, dark blue.

She pointed to the bar and the small stage as she continued to talk to someone blocked by the kitchen door. I took the opportunity to stare at her full, cherry-red lips. I experienced a rude awakening when the door opened wider and revealed the other participant in her animated conversation.

Like I'd been dowsed with a bucket of cold water, I jerked to attention and watched through narrowed eyes as James Brogan, former alderman and newly announced candidate for US Congress, sauntered into the dining area.

My lip curled into a sneer. The man was a piece of work. For a guy his age, the tan was too perfect, the hair too thick, and the face too smooth. He acted like he owned the joint, opening doors and inspecting the bar supplies while his manicured hand stroked the redheaded beauty's arm.

My jaw clenched. Guys like Brogan made me sick. I'd seen my share of them when I carried a shield. They thought the laws didn't apply to them. Fat cat hypocrites dressed in thousand-dollar suits moving through Savannah wheeling and dealing to line their pockets and never giving the citizens and their needs a passing thought.

Of all the fat cats I'd encountered, Brogan was the worst. I couldn't prove it yet, but I knew in my gut the guy was a thief and probably a murderer.

I straightened as the two of them walked by on their way to the door. I nodded to Brogan, careful to keep my expression neutral though I needn't have bothered. The asshole showed no sign that he even recognized me. Why should he? Ruining a man's career was just another day at the office for a prick like him.

My breath caught as the café owner stood on tiptoe and pressed the stars of my most recent fantasy to Brogan's cheek. My gut rolled. The girl I'd gotten hot and bothered over was, in all likelihood, my nemesis' mistress.

Brogan was enjoying the attention, he grinned like a cat with a bowl full of cream as she flashed him her hundred-watt smile and clung to his arm.

I shook my head. The witch wasn't even trying to conceal her affection for the old man, and she had to know the guy was married. It was disgusting. He was old enough to be her father, maybe even her grandfather. I couldn't believe I'd almost asked her out. Talk about near misses.

I tried to close my ears to their conversation, but her words captured my full attention. I watched as she leaned one lushly rounded hip against the door and clutched Brogan's hand. "I'll come by soon, Jamie, okay?"

Brogan smile down at her and enclosed her hand in both of his. "That's fine, Darlin'; you've got a lot to do before your grand opening. Don't make me wait too long though, I'll get lonely."

The knot in my stomach twisted tighter as she threw back her head and laughed before wrapping Brogan in a fierce hug.

"Poor man, I think you'll survive a few nights without my company. There'll be time for our games again, once the café is up and running, I promise." She gave the door a shove. "Just don't go replacing me, ya hear?"

Brogan's hearty laugh echoed through the café as he exited.

She flipped the lock and then turned toward me with a bright smile on her lovely face. My mind raced as I searched for a polite way to brush her off. Maybe I could tell her I was needed back at the office and send one of my techs out to make the sale.

The sooner I got out of there the better. I wasn't sure I could hide my contempt much longer. I forced a smile and started to speak but the polite excuse froze on my lips as she offered her hand.

"Mr. Riordan? I'm sorry to keep you waiting. I'm Ivy Michaels."

The air rushed from my lungs as if I'd been sucker-punched. My heart raced and I gasped for breath as I stared, transfixed by the large blue diamond glittering on her finger.

"Mr. Riordan? Are you okay?" Her eyes were wide and filled with concern. *I was right. Her eyes are blue, as vivid a blue as the ring on her finger.*

I met her gaze and nodded while my mind raced. I needed a moment alone. I needed time to think, get control, and figure out what was going on. "Could I," I cleared my throat and tried again. "Could I get a glass of water?"

"Of course! I'll be right back!" She ran across the room and disappeared through the swinging kitchen door.

I took a deep breath and struggled to control the violent emotions roaring through me. I'd know that ring anywhere. It was etched into my memory, burned into my retinas. The thing even haunted my dreams.

I'd searched for it, spending the better part of my two years as a detective trying to find even a hint of its whereabouts. Now, the thing turned up, out of the blue and on the finger of James Brogan's latest toy. I was nobody's fool, and I didn't believe in coincidence, fate, or dumb luck.

My heart slowed back to its natural rhythm as the initial shock subsided. Questions bombarded my jumbled brain, one after another, each clamoring for answers I didn't have.

I knew of Brogan's involvement, had always known it. I'd just needed the evidence to prove it and the ring at least partially fit the bill. *But how did the girl fit into the puzzle?*

I needed to know before I investigated any further.

The kitchen door slammed against the wall as she raced through carrying a bottle of water. Her blue eyes were huge and filled with concern; her thick mass of fiery red hair streaming behind her.

If possible, the witch was even more beautiful in her worry over me, and, despite everything, my traitorous body was responding.

A split second before she reached my side, I made a decision that would hopefully quench my desire and provide the answers I needed for justice to be served.

I drew a deep breath and prepared to present her with my most charming side. I'd take her out, gain her trust, and pump her for information. I couldn't ignore the flicker of pure male satisfaction that ran through me at the thought of poaching on James Brogan's territory.

Ivy

I opened the last box of frozen, free-range chicken pieces and stacked the bags on the freezer shelf, kicked the empty box out the door, and followed close behind. I shivered and stripped off my gloves, glad the last of the freezer inventory was safely stored. I grinned and strode into the kitchen. It'd been a full day and I should be exhausted and longing for my bed. Instead, my mind was whirling, and all of my senses were on alert. Who knew a break-in at my apartment could lead to romance?

"Wipe the goofy grin off your face, girl; you'll make me think someone's snatched the real Ivy."

I laughed and snagged a handful of almonds from Tina's bag. "I don't know what you mean. How am I not acting like the 'real' Ivy?"

Tina smirked and took a swig of root beer. "The 'real' Ivy doesn't accept dates with men she hardly knows, *and* the 'real' Ivy wouldn't be so excited about such a date." Hands on her hips, Tina screwed her face into a mock glare. "Who are you and what have you done with my best friend?"

I shook my head and laughed. "Quit! You make me sound like a man-hater."

Tina's eyebrows rose. "I've known you for almost seven years. I've seen you date two guys and I hooked you up with both." She slid off of her stool and started flipping off the lights. "Admit it," she teased, "This is not like you." She grabbed her bag and walked through the kitchen door. "I'm gonna change then I'll give you a ride home, okay?"

I grinned and walked into the back room to make sure the door was locked, and the security light was on. Finding everything secure, I slipped on my coat and picked up my purse.

Tina knew me well, sometimes better than I knew myself. It was totally out of character for me to go out with a guy that neither I nor my friends knew. The two men Tina had introduced me to had turned out to be jerks. One had cleaned out my savings account and the other had conveniently forgotten to mention his wife and kids. Tina was a great judge of men!

My policy was to steer clear of men. My experiences, coupled with what I'd witnessed in my aunt's life, suggested they weren't to be trusted. They always started out great and ended up duds. My life was full, even though my friends pestered me to get out and enjoy life. I'd chosen to devote my time and energy to my schooling, then to building a work resume, and now to my business. I didn't need a man in my life to be happy.

My opinions about men and my philosophy on life remained unchanged but I had to admit that if any man could persuade me to alter my beliefs it would be Dominic Riordan. I was intensely aware of him the moment he stepped into the café. My stomach had given a crazy flip and I'd found it difficult to keep my train of thought. I'd had to apologize to my godfather more than once while discussing the grand opening plans.

Waiting for Tina to emerge from the bathroom, I rested my cheek against the cold glass of the front door and wondered what the attraction was. With his inky black hair and intense blue eyes, the security company owner was a gorgeous hunk of a man, but that didn't usually sway me. A passing glance, a nod of appreciation, and I was on my way.

I sensed something deeper with him. His eyes held secrets and shadows I wanted to explore. Our brief discussion showed him to be intelligent and witty. He was more than a good cover for GQ.

He had lounged against the wall with a lazy grace, seeming totally at ease as he surveyed me and my café with a proprietary air. It was almost like he owned it and me. Our eyes met and I shivered. His smoky gaze made me feel things I'd tried to suppress and reminded me of longings best forgotten if I wanted to avoid trouble.

Escorting my godfather to the door brought me near enough to read the warmth and appreciation in his eyes and to witness the sudden change that came over him. He went rigid and his eyes turned the color of a stormy sky.

Looking back now, I wondered what I'd done to bring on such an about-face, but as I continued to reflect on that moment, I realized he wasn't looking at me but at James Brogan.

The intensity of that gaze made me pause. I'd considered refusing his dinner invitation, but the attraction was too strong. I did plan to ask about his issue with Jamie though, and I wanted to know what had caused his apparent illness after Jaime left.

White-faced and gasping for air, he'd scared me to death. I was just sure he was going to pass out and bang his head on the concrete floor, yet he was fine when I returned with the water. If he had attacks like that out of the blue, I'd like to be prepared. Maybe he was diabetic or something.

I sighed and rolled my eyes as the door to the bathroom opened and Tina came out looking spiffy in her 'new' vintage outfit. I shook my head. If I was a hippy child, Tina was channeling the Mods. White go-go boots, lime green micro-mini dress, false eyelashes, and thick black eyeliner. The girl had it going on in spades.

"Where are you headed tonight?" I flicked off the lights and held the door open.

Tina grinned and stepped onto the sidewalk. "Wouldn't you like to know?"

I turned the key in the lock and then cocked my eyebrow at Tina. "Yes, as a matter of fact, I would. Dressed like that, you're bound to find trouble ... or cause it, so I think I'd better know which police precinct to find you in."

Tina winked. "Haha, Ivy. Maybe it's you who'll get into trouble tonight. Ya got a hot date, after all."

I rolled my eyes and slid into the passenger seat. "Please. I'm the responsible stick-in-the-mud, remember? I never get into trouble."

Tina snorted and started the engine. "Well, one can always hope."

Head Over Heels

Ivy

I glanced at the clock for the hundredth time before leaning toward the mirror and applying a thin line of black liquid along my upper eyelid. I did the same to the other eye and then stood back to admire the effect. My mouth twisted to the side as I debated my handiwork. Wearing makeup was not my normal custom and I wished I'd let Tina have her way after all. My refusal of Tina's offer was spurred by the fear that my exuberant friend would paint me up like a three-dollar tart but looking like a clown was not any better and perhaps a good deal worse.

I sighed and scrubbed the inky stuff off. Maybe some more of the dark plum shadow I'd smoothed along the brow bone would serve better; it certainly couldn't look any worse. A dusting of powder and a flick of mascara and I decided to leave well enough alone. Dominic Riordan would just have to take me the way I was because I wasn't, and never would be, a girly girl. I strode to the closet and scanned the row of colorful fabrics. But I did like pretty dresses and had a collection of them.

I sorted through an array of bright, gauzy dresses and pulled out my favorite. I fingered the soft purple and green swirled fabric and debated the choice. The tiny straps and thin material weren't suited for a winter evening along the river, but if I added a pair of black tights and a purple bolero jacket, it should be warm enough. I pulled the dress over my head and turned to root through my dresser drawer.

"Crap!" Underwear, socks, and bras went flying to the floor as the clock in the living room chimed the quarter-hour. I sat on the side of the bed and shoved one foot into the stockings.

"Meeow!" I looked up as Sergeant trotted into the bedroom demanding dinner. "I'll feed you in a minute, learn some patience." I slipped my foot into the other leg of the tights and stood to pull them over my hips. The cat twirled around my feet. "Quit Sergeant! You're gonna get white hair all over my legs!"

I nudged the cat aside and ran back to the closet. My shoulders fell. The closet floor was a mess of shoes, belts, purses, and who knew what else. I couldn't remember the last time I'd worn my one pair of heels and Lord only knew where they were hiding. I signed and dropped to my knees. Sergeant promptly joined me, mewling and rubbing in his attempts to entice a can of food out of me. I resigned myself to my fate and hoped I knew where the lint brush was or at least a roll of tape.

Five long minutes later and just as the doorbell rang, I managed to locate a pair of black half-boots; they'd just have to do. A quick check in the hall mirror showed me looking more frazzled than I liked but there was nothing for it. Again, he'd have to take me as is or take a hike. I pasted what I hoped was a serene smile onto my face, pushed the now howling cat away with my foot, and opened the door.

Dom

My gut clenched as I looked down at Ivy's flushed face and bright eyes. She was gorgeous- obviously flustered, but gorgeous. I checked my watch. "Am I early? We did say six so I could go over the house and determine your security needs, right?"

A panicked look flashed in her eyes for a second before she smiled and stepped aside. I wondered at it but decided she was just running late. A glance at the living room revealed goldish green walls, black and beige furniture, lots of plants, and the wide white woodwork typical of eighteenth-century houses.

I smiled. For an earth child and neo-hippy, the apartment was decidedly calm in décor, very Zen; I could kick back in a place like that.

A strident whine drew my gaze to the back of the sofa where a fluffy white cat with startling blue eyes perched. I ran my hand down the cat's back then scratched its chubby cheeks as it emitted a loud purr. The door clicked shut and Ivy came up behind me.

"Pretty cat, what's its nam- "

"Oh, don't pet him- "

"Ouch!" A deep growl, a flash of white, and a burning sensation on the top of my hand said her warning had come a second too late.

I yanked my hand away and stared at the white bit of fluff as it turned into a demon. Ears flat against its huge head, it opened its mouth wide and bared its teeth before hissing and running from the room. On second thought, maybe I wouldn't want to kick back there.

"Sergeant Pepper, bad kitty! I'm so sorry. Here, let me see." Ivy took my hand.

I swore under my breath as every part of my body jumped to attention. The feel of her soft fingers running over the back of my hand was driving me to distraction.

She grabbed a tissue and blotted at the speck of blood, and then bit her lip and looked at me from beneath long, sooty black lashes.

"Does it hurt? I have some peroxide."

I shook my head, trying to clear it. "No, it's fine. Just a scratch." I jerked my gaze away from her beguiling eyes. "What'd I do to make it attack?" Not that I cared, but I needed to focus before I did something I'd regret.

She gave a little giggle that curled my toes. I stifled a groan. The girl was going to drive me mad. I'd have to be on guard, or I'd fall for her and forget all about my search for answers and quest for justice.

"Nothing actually; Sergeant just isn't partial to men." She cocked her head to one side and the corner of her oh-so-kissable mouth twitched. "To most humans honestly. I uh ... I am sorry. I should get a bandage, don't you think?"

Preoccupied, I didn't immediately answer. She started to fidget under my scrutiny, and I stared, mesmerized by the action of her small white teeth nibbling on her lower lip. She was so close I could smell the fruity scent of the glossy stuff on her lips, the full red lips that had haunted me since I'd left the café that afternoon.

God! I gritted my teeth and fought for control. I concentrated on her perfidy, on her involvement with Brogan, on her wearing the diamond. My eyes widened as I glanced at her bare right hand.

I shook my head. "I'm fine. No need for a bandage." I removed my hand from hers and strove to keep my voice casual. "What happened to that ring you were wearing earlier, the big blue one?"

She blinked. "Huh?" She looked down at her hand. "Oh! You noticed that? I guess I forgot to put it back on after I showered. Thanks for reminding me, I need to grab some earrings, too. The ring is just old costume jewelry but wearing it makes me feel good."

"Oh. Sure looked real to me. Thought it might have been a family heirloom or something." I shrugged and tried to sound unconcerned while the wheels in my head turned.

Her confession irritated me. I didn't want a present of Brogan's making her feel good and that it mattered at all bothered me even more.

Putting my personal feelings aside, she appeared to be telling the truth about the ring, yet I found it hard to believe she didn't know its value. Would she *really* accept a piece of glass from a lover as wealthy as Brogan?

I couldn't put my finger on it, but I knew in my gut that something wasn't right. She had to know about the ring if she was involved the way I suspected. I shook off my doubts and walked to the bank of windows. I'd push for more answers over dinner.

"This courtyard go with your place?"

The rustle of her dress and the faint smell of a sweet perfume announced her presence. "Yes, all the tenants can use it but mine is the only one with direct access."

I nodded and turned to survey the room. "How about showing me around before we go? I need to see all the points of entry before I can give you a quote on the security system."

She flashed a hesitant smile. "Sure ... uh, just ignore the mess, okay? I was planning to pick up before you arrived."

I grinned. That must have been the reason for her panic when I arrived. "No problem. I don't charge extra for the mess, though I might have to for that cat. Have to give my techs hazard pay."

She giggled and walked toward the hall. "Sergeant is all right; he just has issues."

I snorted. "Issues? With that animal around, you don't need an alarm system."

She laughed and opened the door to the right of the living room. "This is the guest room and my office." She stepped back for me to enter.

I glanced around the small room, noting the corner window that looked out over an alley. She'd divided the room using filing cabinets and low bookshelves. The side holding the daybed and nightstand were in perfect order, but papers lay scattered across the glass top of her desk, covering her laptop. The center drawer lay in pieces on the floor and the front of one filing cabinet was smashed in.

I looked at her, eyebrows raised. "I assume your burglars hit this room?"

She grinned. "Yes, I'm not this disorganized."

"They take all the electronics?"

Ivy looked around the room and frowned. "No, actually. I don't think they took anything. Obviously, they went through my papers. I haven't had time for a thorough search, but from what I can tell, they just rooted around and broke some things. They also went through my jewelry box and my dressing table, though I can't find anything missing in there, either." She shrugged. "Maybe it was just kids."

I nodded and motioned her out of the room. "Could have been kids, but sensors on all windows and doors will ensure they don't come back. I want to make sure you're safe."

Her lips formed a shy smile. She moved down the short hallway. "Thanks. It's creepy, knowing someone was in here looking through my things." She looked over her shoulder. "I had a hard time sleeping last night."

"You'll sleep easier once the alarm is in place. There's a panic button on the box and a direct link intercom to our call station, so if anything should happen while you're here, just push the button and yell. We'll hear you."

She stopped before a closed door and turned toward me, her eyes huge and her face white. "Oh God, don't say that! I don't know what I'd do if someone broke in while I was here; that's every single woman's nightmare!"

She reached for the doorknob, and I noticed her hand trembling. I swore under my breath and laid a hand on her shoulder, turning her back toward me.

Her gaze was fixed on the floor. I tipped her chin up and scanned her face, noting her eyes were bright with unshed tears. My thumb rubbed along her jaw as our eyes locked, "Don't be afraid, I'll keep you safe."

Her lip quivered and tears overflowed, running down her cheeks. I flicked them away and stroked my fingers along her delicate jaw. Her skin was like silk beneath my hand. Her head tilted to one side, and I watched as her tongue peeped out to moisten her full lips.

I swallowed hard and fought the urge to press mine to hers. Everything about her drew me like a magnet and made every nerve-ending hum. My body screamed to move closer, to draw her into my arms.

I shook my head in an attempt to rein in my thoughts. No matter my attraction, I had to get a grip. The mission was too vital, the answers I sought, too important. I had to get proof Brogan was guilty of insurance fraud, and possibly murder, and I had to do it before the bastard was elected to Congress. God knew the country didn't need any more criminals in Washington.

I lowered my hand and stepped back. "Sorry, I didn't mean to ... you get to me."

She searched my eyes as if looking for the truth. She must have been satisfied because a timid smile shaped her rosy lips. "You get to me, too."

My gut twisted at her mumbled confession. I'd intended to pump her for information, not to form a relationship. Things were getting complicated.

I cleared my throat and looked at my watch. "How about showing me the rest of the apartment? I made a reservation for seven at Vic's."

She blushed and gave a nervous laugh. "Oh, yeah we should get going." She turned the knob and pushed the door open, stepping aside for me to enter. "This is my room."

She walked over to a dresser and slipped the blue diamond onto her finger, then leaned toward the mirror and fiddled with a pair of hoop earrings while nodding to her right. "That archway leads to the bathroom and closet and those are the only windows."

I nodded and looked to where she'd pointed. Two windows and French doors occupied one wall. I could just make out a black wrought iron balcony and a spiral staircase leading down to the garden.

My lips twitched as I looked over the rest of the master suite. Here was the hippy child. Sunshine yellow walls, lined with framed album covers from the sixties, tie-dyed curtains, and a black bedspread with bright orange and green pillows. Judging by her room and the café, she had a thing for the psychedelic.

I made a mental note of the windows and doors and decided to have a keypad mounted on the wall beside her bed. "All done in here; show me the rest."

We walked through the kitchen where I counted three more windows, then down a flight of stairs to a glassed-in porch that made me groan. The room was a burglar's fantasy. Six large picture windows and a flimsy excuse for a door, also glass. No amount of alarms could make that room secure.

I chose my words carefully. If I scared her again, we'd never make it to dinner. "Ivy, this room isn't designed for an alarm system."

She frowned.

"See, for the sensors to work, the window has to be a casement- never mind, just know that the window has to be lifted for the alarm to sound. These windows are stationary, so the sensors won't work."

She bit her lip. "So, you're saying I can't monitor this room?"

"Not exactly. We can install a door sensor, but if someone wants in, all they'll have to do is break the glass."

I saw fear growing in her eyes and moved quickly to reassure her. "Here's what I think we should do. I'll have my techs over first thing in the morning to install door and window sensors on everything on the main floor. Down here, we'll put a sensor on the outside door and another on the interior door that leads to the stairs. That way, even if they get in through a window, the interior door alarm, will go off. The only other thing we can do is set up a closed-circuit camera and laser sensors, but I think that's overkill."

I grinned and flicked the end of her nose. "You're not keeping the crown jewels here and you do have that attack cat."

She smiled, although her eyes still showed concern. "You're the expert; I'll go with what you suggest."

I followed as she turned and started up the stairs. A minute later, my stomach flipped as she stopped and looked over her shoulder.

"I trust you."

Too Close for Comfort

Dom

I smiled as Ivy finished giving the waiter our order. She was in her element at the four-star restaurant, discussing the menu, asking what was new, which chef was working, and other things that only a chef who'd worked there would think to ask.

After several of the staff had dropped by our table to congratulate her on the Cosmic Café and the waiter left with our order, I reached across the table and clasped her hand. Her blue eyes were filled with happiness and her smile was infectious.

"Seems I made a good choice in restaurants. It never occurred to me that you might have worked here."

Ivy's smile widened. "Oh, you did pick a great place! I worked here until about six months ago when I decided to open the café, and this is the first time I've been back."

She looked around the dining room and then nodded toward a set of dark oak doors. "I worked in that kitchen for three years. I started as a prep chef and was assistant to the executive chef before I left."

Her gaze returned to me, and I noted her expression had changed. Tears swam and threatened to spill from her eyes.

"Hey, what's the matter? The way you greeted everyone I assumed you had enjoyed working here. Would you rather leave?"

Ivy gave a choked little laugh and sniffed. "No, oh no. I'm just being silly. When Vic and Chef Paul hired me, they took a chance on a young know-nothing just out of school, and ... well, these people were like my family. I guess now that I have no real family ... it's just hitting me hard. I'm sorry, don't mind me." She pushed her chair back from the table and gave him a watery smile. "I'd better go to the restroom and make sure I don't look like a raccoon."

"You look beautiful, but I know you won't take my word for it!" I squeezed her hand and then stood. "Hurry back."

She flashed another sweet smile and continued across the hardwood floor, disappearing through an alcove. I resumed my seat and stared out the tall window beside me. I watched the ripple of the river's current while I formulated a plan to find the answers I sought. She'd volunteered information about her family already. My quarry was making the job easy.

I rose and held her chair as Ivy came back to the table. "Everything all right now?"

Ivy replaced her napkin on her lap. "Yes. I'm, fine. Don't mind me. Good, grief tears twice in less than two hours. I'm not usually this emotional, I swear."

I took her hand, rubbing my thumb in lazy circles across the top of it and enjoying the silkiness of her skin. A dozen questions raced through my mind, but I'd have to tread carefully, or she'd end up crying in the restroom again.

"I don't think you're overly emotional. You have a lot on your mind right now. Opening a business is stressful and a break-in didn't help matters."

Ivy nodded. "I'll say. I never thought it'd be so complicated. I'm a chef so how hard can it be to set up a kitchen and start cooking? The worst part has been all the paperwork. Federal and state tax ID numbers, sales tax forms, health department permits, ugh! But that isn't what has me so upset." She took a deep breath. "Last Thursday, the police found my aunt in the Savannah River."

My eyes widened. Not what I'd been expecting. "God! I read about that in the paper, but I didn't realize ..." I squeezed her hand. "I'm sorry, Ivy. So now you're dealing with a funeral."

"Kind of. She wanted to be cremated, and since I'm the only family and she didn't have any friends here, it was a simple funeral-just me and my godfather."

"Oh, so you do have some type of family. Has he been there for you?"

A radiant smile lit her face and I knew a moment of jealousy that it wasn't for me. "Oh yes, I couldn't ask for better. Jamie has been like a father to me."

"Jamie?"

"Umm, James Brogan."

My hand clenched around hers as I sucked in a breath. She wasn't his mistress but his goddaughter!

Ivy frowned and pulled her hand away. "Is something wrong?"

I swallowed hard and forced a smile. "No, not at all." I reached for her hand again. "I'm sorry, did I squeeze too hard?" I rubbed the top of her hand. "I'm just surprised, that's all. Your godfather is a powerful guy."

Ivy bit her lip and looked out at the river. "Yes, he is. I couldn't help but notice your reaction when you saw him this afternoon at the Cosmic. Do you two know each other?"

I gave a shaky laugh. The girl was perceptive, or my poker face was rusty. "I know him, but I doubt he remembers me. I ran afoul of him over an investigation I was conducting when I was a detective."

Ivy turned from the window in surprise. "I didn't know you'd been a cop!" She laughed. "Stupid of me. We just met so really we don't know much about each other at all!"

I grinned. She was making my job incredibly easy. "You're right, so how about telling me your life story?"

Laughter bubbled from her lips and her eyes were once more sparkling. "Oh no, I promise my life is not that interesting. I'd rather hear about your experiences on the force."

I shrugged. "Nothing much to tell, being a cop isn't as excit-" I released her hand as the waiter arrived with our meal. My mouth watered as the aroma of herbs and lemon reached my nose. "Wow, this looks great."

Ivy smiled and picked up her knife and fork. "Vic's is famous for its baked flounder." She popped a bit of the flaky white fish into her mouth and closed her eyes. "Ummm, this is wonderful. The fish is moist, but firm, and the sauce is a perfect balance of lemon, white pepper, and herbs de Provence. Do you taste that zingy note at the end?" She licked her lips and opened her eyes. "You haven't taken a bite!"

I laughed. "I was too busy watching you!" I grinned and took a bite. "Man, this is great, but what is that flavor, it's kind of ..."

Ivy laughed. "You do taste it! You have a good palate. That slightly floral note is lavender."

I frowned. "The flower? I didn't know you could cook with that!"

"Yep, it's the mystery ingredient in the French herbs de Provence. Do you like it?"

I nodded. "Yeah, it's interesting." I took a sip of wine. "So, back to your life story, tell me everything."

Ivy shook her head and swallowed. "Not much to tell really. I was born in Savannah and lived here until I was nine. My parents were killed in a car crash and my dad's sister, Fey raised me."

"And that's the aunt that just died? So, you've no other family?"

Ivy took another bite before answering. "No, I'm the last. I'm sure there is some distant family somewhere but I've no idea who they may be. Aunt Fey never talked about family. She lived in the moment."

I searched her face looking for telltale signs that she resented my probing. My interrogation skills were serving me well. She seemed perfectly comfortable with my questions and showed no signs that she thought my curiosity suspicious. "You said you lived here until you were nine, so where did you live after that?"

Her eyes twinkled and her mouth spread into a wide smile. "Where haven't I lived would be a better question." She sipped her wine. "About a month after my parents died, Aunt Fey came into my room one morning and told me to pack a bag. We left Savannah on the twelfth of August 1992, and I didn't return until I graduated from college." She laughed. "Among other, less noteworthy places, I've lived on an Indian reservation in Oklahoma, a new-age commune in Oregon, and an artist's colony in Virginia."

I took a deep breath and struggled to keep my expression blank. She'd left town two days after my mother was murdered. More coincidences: they were stacking up. I filed the information and then focused on her remarks. I snorted and set my fork down. "Are you kidding?"

She giggled. "Nope. My aunt was ... hmmm, let's be charitable and say she was free-spirited and free with her love. She had a lot of boyfriends and they led her to an adventurous life."

I shook my head and laughed "I'll say. My childhood was not nearly so interesting."

Ivy leaned across the table and smiled. "Do tell."

When I shook my head, she raised her eyebrows and smirked. "I emptied my closet; now it's your turn, fess up."

I laughed and held up my hands. "All right, I surrender and confess all." I took my last bite of fish and then pushed the plate aside. "Not much to tell and certainly not as interesting as your tale. I was born here and lived in Savannah for twelve years until my mother died, then I moved to Darien and lived with my dad."

Ivy's smile dimmed. "We have something in common then, huh? We both know what it's like to lose parents at a young age. What is Darien like? I've driven past it on my way to Saint Simon's but never went into the town."

"Darien? Well, it's a fishing village mostly. Just about everyone is or knows someone, in the shrimp business. Dad was a shrimper."

Her eyes widened. "Really? How neat. Did you go out with him? Is it anything like that show about the fishermen in Alaska?"

I laughed. "You have a vivid imagination. No, it isn't anything like crabbing in Alaska except that you're on a boat and it stinks like fish. Shrimping isn't a bad way to make a living but it's not the most reliable way either. Some years were good, and others were downright awful. It all depended on the season." I signaled the waiter for the check. "I got tired of the long days at sea and decided early on that it wasn't for me."

"Is that why you decided to become a policeman?"

I looked out the window and watched a cargo ship work its way up the river. I swallowed hard and forced myself to speak the words that seemed to stick in my throat, almost as if, by not speaking the truth it would alter it. "I joined the force because my mother was murdered, and the crime was never solved."

Ivy gasped. "Oh Dom, I'm so sorry."

I searched her face, and read the contrition and sympathy written there. I looked down at the blue diamond sparkling on her finger. Would she still feel that way when I proved the great James Brogan was responsible and that she was the key to proving it?

Doubtful, which was why I reminded myself, that I needed to keep my head. A relationship with Ivy Michaels could go nowhere; time to take back the interrogation and get on with my plans.

I forced a smile. "It was a long time ago. You never get over it, but you do move on, I promise."

She smiled and then looked down at our joined hands. "I believe you, or at least my head does. My heart won't let me forget that Aunt Fey died violently, and we never really made amends." She sniffed. "She never got over my moving back here."

I squeezed her hand and then stood. "Let's get out of here, hmm? Clear our heads and get rid of our gloomy thoughts."

Ivy swiped at her eyes then smiled and rose from her seat. "Yes, let's have some fun."

I helped her into her jacket and then guided her from the restaurant. The mellow sounds of an acoustic guitar reached our ears as we stepped out onto the sidewalk. Ivy looked up and grinned. "Sounds like a friend of mine is playing at the No Quarter Saloon. Want to stop in?"

I nodded. "Sounds good."

We set off toward the old cotton warehouse. "Do you go here often?"

Ivy shook her head. "No, not much anymore. When I worked the night shift at Vic's, a couple of us would stop in after closing, but since I started planning my café, I've been too busy."

We climbed the steep steps and showed our IDs to the large man guarding the door. Music engulfed us as we walked inside.

"Little darlin' ..."

I turned my gaze toward the stage. A dark-haired man was perched on a stool, strumming a guitar. He nodded at us and then sang, "...and Ivy's here so ... it's all right."

Ivy laughed and gave him a wave before heading to an empty table where we ordered drinks. The music was too loud for conversation, so I sat back and watched her. From the singer on the stage to the bartender and servers, it was evident she was a regular and popular patron. Just like at the restaurant, everyone seemed to love her.

I couldn't blame them. Her smile was contagious, drawing people like moths to a flame. Logic pointed out that someone as well-liked as Ivy couldn't be guilty of what I suspected.

My conscience smote me for what I intended, but I suppressed it. I knew in my gut she was the key to every-thing, and I had to proceed. The goal was too important. I just hoped she'd forgive me if she were as innocent as she appeared.

The familiar opening of a classic rock song brought me from my reverie. I downed the remainder of my drink and thought the song choice was appropriate. Since meeting Ivy that morning, I'd known nothing but pressure.

I looked down at the ring sparkling on her finger. We'd talked all night and I still didn't know how she came by the ring. The last notes rang out and the singer an-nounced a short break.

I pushed my chair away from the table and stood. It was time for more subtle questioning and a loud pub wasn't the venue.

Ivy looked up and smiled. "Had enough?"

I threw a tip onto the table. "He's great but yea, it's getting late, and tomorrow is a workday."

Her mouth curved into a rueful grimace. "Yep, tomorrow is another long day at the Cosmic for me. Just let me tell Thomas goodbye and we'll go."

I stood by the door and watched her laugh at something the singer said. My jaw tightened as the guy wrapped his arms around her and planted a kiss on her cheek. There were entirely too many men at liberty to touch her for my satisfaction.

Once again, my conscience chose to remind me that my intentions weren't completely honorable, and I hadn't any right to be jealous. That didn't ease the knot in my chest.

She turned and gave me a bright smile as she worked her way through the crowd. I thought again about how quickly I could lose my heart to her. She was beautiful, intelligent, and incredibly sweet.

Just my luck that the woman of my dreams was wrapped several layers deep in the event which consumed my life. I smiled and took her hand to maneuver the narrow stairs. The sooner I finished the investigation the better for all concerned.

Ivy

I clutched Dom's hand and picked my way across the cobblestones. I shivered as a gust of wind pulled at my jacket, then smiled as he wrapped his arm around me, pulling me close to his side.

So far, the evening had been the best date of my life. From the moment he'd picked me up, Dom was charm itself. He opened my car door, held my chair, and concerned himself with my comfort. Maybe I'd finally found a keeper. Who knew all I'd had to do was get robbed to find a decent guy?

"What are you smiling at?"

I looked up and grinned. "Can't tell you, I'd jinx myself."

Dom laughed. "That sounds ominous." He steered me across River Street toward the boardwalk. "Are you warm enough to walk along the river?"

I nodded. "Um-hmm, I love to watch the river at night. It's so cool to see the ships come in all lit up."

"I like it, too."

We strolled along in easy silence, pausing to watch a couple of street musicians before heading toward a quieter end of the strip. We leaned against the concrete railing and watched a cargo ship make its way to the port.

Another gust of wind made me shiver and draw my free hand into the sleeve of my jacket. I felt a tug on my finger and sighed. "Crap!"

I removed my hand from Dom's and tried to unwind the threads of my coat from the ring.

Dom looked down. "What's wrong?"

I fiddled with the tangled threads. "Oh, it's this ring. There must be a prong loose or else it's just the setting. Either way, it keeps getting caught on things."

I worked the ring loose and slipped my hand back into his. "I've already managed to pull a snag in my favorite sweater. I guess I'd better quit wearing it."

Dom grasped my wrist and drew my hand up so that the ring shone in the streetlight. "Something this valuable, you'd be better to have it repaired. You wouldn't want the stone to fall out."

I chuckled and slipped my hand back up the sleeve. "It's just a sentimental thing. I don't think it's worth much, but I would hate to lose it just the same."

Dom nodded. "Where'd you get it?"

"The ring?" I smiled. "It belonged to my aunt, or at least I think it did."

Dom frowned. "You think?"

I laughed. "Yeah, with my aunt, you never know. Still, I found it at the bottom of a safety deposit box, along with some old pictures of our family and stuff, so I'm assuming it was Aunt Fey's. Probably something one of her boyfriends gave her." I looked up at him and grinned. "That's why I doubt it is anything but pretty glass. I never knew my aunt to date a man capable of buying anything real." I shrugged. "Besides, what gem is this color of blue naturally? It's too light to be a sapphire and I've never seen an aquamarine this clear."

"It could be a diamond. The Hope is blue like that."

I threw my head back and laughed. "Oh yeah, I can just see Aunt Fey with the Hope diamond."

Dom didn't return my grin. He searched my face, his eyes intent. "Stranger things have happened, but I didn't say it was *the* Hope diamond, just that it's the same color of blue."

I broke eye contact and looked out at the river. "Nah, it has to be glass. It's pretty glass, but still, just glass."

I looked up in time to see a strange expression on Dom's face, a cross between exasperation and irritation, and the whole tinged with suspicion like I was lying or had something to hide. I frowned, wondering what had caused it. The easy camaraderie of the night seemed to have slipped away, and for the first time, I felt uncomfortable. The way he watched me now reminded me of the detectives who'd come to tell me about my aunt. I shook my head. Perhaps all cops, even former ones, had that look. Maybe they taught it at the academy.

I looked up as he laughed. The intent expression was gone, and I wondered if I'd imagined it.

Dom shrugged. "Well, whatever it is, you should get it fixed since it means so much to you." He gave my hand a gentle tug. "Shall we go?"

I looked at my watch and nodded. "Yeah, I'd best get home. Lots of deliveries tomorrow. I'm so excited about my grand opening!"

"What do you have planned?"

I chattered about the plans for opening night as we walked along the now deserted waterfront. We slowed as we neared the shadowed alley that led to Factor's Walk, allowing me time to pick my way across the jumbled cobblestones.

I gave a rueful laugh. "I'm sorry. I thought these boots would be easier to walk in down here, but they are just as bad as high heels!"

I tripped on a loose stone and Dom caught me, turning so our bodies were flush. His arms wrapped around my waist. "Easy now, don't want you to twist an ankle."

I caught my breath at the feel of his tall, hard body pressed against mine. There was no doubt he wanted me, and God help me, I wanted him, too.

I swallowed hard and wrestled with the voice in my head that insisted on pointing out what I already knew. They'd only known each other a few hours and I'd be a fool to rush in, especially with my track record. But my heart said Dom was different. He understood a childhood of loneliness and isolation. He'd felt the pain and vulnerability that came from losing a parent. They connected. I trusted him. He made me feel safe and cherished. It was time to take a chance. Pushing the last of my doubts aside, I leaned closer and licked my lips. My stomach fluttered in anticipation as he lowered his lips to mine.

I swayed as he nibbled at my lower lip and traced its fullness with the tip of his tongue. A shiver, that owed nothing to the cold, ran through me and I parted my lips and then gasped as his tongue swept inside, exploring and mating with mine. I moaned and wrapped my arms around his neck, surrendering to the sensations coursing through me.

Dom pulled his lips from mine and trailed a line of kisses across my cheek and whispered in my ear. "I've wanted to do that all night."

I gave a breathless laugh. "Then why didn't you?"

He groaned and took my lips again. I squirmed and returned the kiss, lost to all rational thought.

"Now ain't this nice?"

The snide remark from behind me was like a slap in the face, shocking me from my stupor. I felt Dom stiffen as he raised his head and looked over my shoulder.

At Cross Purposes

Dom

My arms tightened around Ivy as I peered at the man standing directly behind her. His face was in shadow, both from lack of light and the dark hood of his jacket, but I saw enough to know he meant trouble. The hairs on the back of my neck rose.

I pushed Ivy behind me. "Stay behind me and be quiet."

Ivy whimpered, her eyes were wide and filled with fear. I squeezed her hand and then turned my full attention to the man standing before me. Something in his hand gleamed in the moonlight, and without thought, my hand went to my side, looking for the gun that used to be there.

The other man's gaze followed my movements. "Don't play the hero, big man; just give me what I want, and we'll call it a night."

I gritted my teeth. "And just what is it you want?"

The man smirked. "Well now, how's about handing over the little lady's ring? I'm takin' a fancy to it."

My eyes narrowed as a light bulb went off in my brain-the break-in at Ivy's house with nothing missing and now an attempted mugging with no demand for money.

They weren't coincidences. Someone and I was pretty sure who, wanted the blue diamond on Ivy's finger and they wanted it badly. Looked like they would be disappointed, again.

My hands clenched into fists, and I shifted my weight to the balls of my feet. "How about you go to hell."

No sooner had the words left my mouth than the man's arm was swinging toward me. A flash of metal revealed a long, wicked-looking blade.

Ivy screamed as I sprang forward and caught the attacker's wrist, bending it backward and dragging the man closer. A sickening crunch rent the air as my foot slammed into the guy's knee, sending him tumbling onto the hard stones.

I kicked the knife away and pivoted toward Ivy. "Get up the steps, now!"

Ivy scrambled to obey, and I turned back to the would-be attacker, mewling on the ground. I leaned over until our eyes met. "Tell your boss he'd better send a real man to do his dirty work next time."

Ivy

I clung to the wrought iron rail and watched Dom climb the narrow stairs. I shook my head and marveled that he could be so calm. I was shaking so hard my legs barely supported me. I bit my lip to keep my teeth from chattering and drew deep breaths to calm my racing heart.

"Are you all, right?" Dom crossed to my side and wrapped an arm around my waist. I managed a nod and leaned into him, grateful for his strength.

"Come on, let's get you out of here."

I looked back over my shoulder to see the attacker dragging himself toward a parked car before Dom tugged on my arm. I shuddered, thinking of what might have happened had he not been with me. I turned away, gripping Dom's arm and forcing my legs to move.

I stumbled along beside him then stopped. Choking back the bile stinging my throat, I stammered, "What about him? Shouldn't we call the police or an ambulance?"

Dom stiffened and his voice was dry as he replied, "I think it's best if we don't get involved. He'll scurry back under whichever rock he crawled out from."

My eyes widened as words tumbled from my mouth in a rush. "Dom! You were a policeman, I don't understand. That guy had a knife and he tried to rob us. If we don't report it, he might do it again to someone else!"

"Ivy ...," Dom gripped my shoulders, giving me a little shake. "Normally, I'd do as you suggest but, despite common sense I find I like you ..."

"Wha ...?"

I bit back a response as he dragged a hand through his hair and exhaled, though it did little to relieve his tension. I gasped at the expression on his face. He was furious, a muscle ticking in his cheek from clenching his teeth. I frowned, that anger seemed to be directed at me!

"Look, not the time or place, we need to get out of here before they come back." He grabbed my arm and set a brisk pace towards the car. "We can figure out how to get your pretty ass out of this once we're safe."

I let him propel me forward, stumbling to keep up as my mind whirled. Out of what? He liked me *despite* himself? My shock and fear turned to bewildered anger and I jerked to a stop, pulling Dom off balance.

He swore under his breath and glared at me. "What now?"

I glared right back. "What did you mean, get my ass out of this?" I ignored the smidge of salve to my vanity that he'd referred to it as a pretty one and stayed focused. "How is a random mugging my fault?"

Dom clamped his lips shut and breathed through his nose, giving me the distinct impression, that he was counting to control his temper. Well, tough! I was rapidly building to that level of frustration, too. I was the victim here, we both were! So why was he attacking me?

We glared at each other, putting me in mind of a warped game of chicken. A car went by, loud exhaust competing with the thud of a sub-woofer breaking our standoff. I rolled my eyes and took a step back. "Look, let's just file this in the dud folder and call it a night." I looked around, taking in the nearly deserted Bay Street, and decided to return to the No Quarter and beg a ride. No way I was comfortable walking the five blocks to my home now.

I backed away. "Thanks for dinner and, well everything …" I snorted at my lameness and rushed on, eager to put an end to another crap date. Would I ever pick a keeper? I shook off the depressing answer from my subconscious and gave a half-wave towards Dom over my shoulder. "Goodnig- hey!" Dom's fingers fastened around my upper arm, stopping me in my tracks. "What the-"

"You're not going anywhere but with me, Ivy."

My eyes widened and a frisson of fear curled in my belly. Was he going to turn nasty? Was he crudely thinking I owed him after that dinner? He'd seemed like a gentleman but then, I did know how to pick them.

I straightened and settled my weight evenly on both feet. He might be big, but I knew where to kick. "Let go of me, please. I think we've reached the end of our date."

Denied flight, my body was prepared for a fight, so the last thing I expected from Dom was a bark of laughter, an arm tossed over my shoulder in a gentle, friendly half hug, and a nudge to start walking. "Baby, the date is definitely over!"

He laughed again, though I thought it sounded self-mocking. "Gorgeous and sexy you may be, but you'll have to forgive me if I can't see my way past theft, fraud, and murder. I'm old-fashioned like that."

He opened the car door, and I was so confused, so shocked, so exhausted from the whirl of emotional changes I'd cycled through over the past thirty minutes that I let him bundle me into the seat without protest.

"Buckle up."

I stared at him as he started the car.

He snorted and leaned across, fastening my seat belt before setting the vehicle into motion. "You're in shock, just sit back and breathe, we'll be home soon."

Despite his nonsensical statements and misplaced anger, I had to acknowledge that I didn't feel threatened by him, and he was likely right, I was in shock. I leaned back against the headrest and closed my eyes, trying to calm my nerves on the short ride to my house.

Nothing seemed quite real. Things like this didn't happen to people like me. I'd always lived such a quiet and uneventful life, at least since moving out on my own.

I bit back a sob and tried to calm myself. I'd run the gamut of emotions over the last week and my body was finally responding to the overload. I couldn't think straight and all I wanted to do was curl into a fetal position and have a good cry.

Dom

I spared a glance at Ivy's white face as I raced the car down Island's Expressway. I couldn't decide if she was going to faint or throw up. Given a choice, I'd choose the former.

Her reaction to the night's excitement suggested she wasn't used to being in a den of thieves, despite what I'd implied to her. She'd been a child when the theft and murder had occurred, there was no way she was responsible and she was either an Oscar-worthy actress, a sociopath without conscience, or as naïve as a kitten when it came to her godfather.

After spending the evening with her, I'd put good money on the latter, but where did that leave my investigation? Not quite back to square one since I knew the whereabouts of the ring, but it was now obvious Brogan did, too. It was also clear that he wasn't letting anything, even his relationship with Ivy, stand in the way of gaining possession of it.

Her safety was now a definite issue, maybe her life. I had no choice but to trust her with the whole story and hope my instincts were sound and that her sense of self-preservation would outweigh her loyalty to the man who'd been, in her words, "like a father" to her. Otherwise, we'd both end up dead.

I maneuvered a curve and then slowed the car to the main drag's speed limit before reaching for her hand. I looked over as she tightened her grip. Her eyes remained closed, but her lips were forming silent words in time to the rhythmic rise and fall of her chest.

I smirked, suspecting she was meditating or chanting mantras, just like a good little hippy chick. I left her in peace; a calm suspect, or witness as I now leaned towards categorizing her, made my job easier.

The tires crunched on the sand and gravel road that led to my house and Ivy jerked upright and stared, wide-eyed. "What ... where are we?"

So much for calm. I pulled into the carport and killed the engine before turning towards her and releasing her seat belt. "We are on Tybee; I brought you to my place."

Ivy gasped. "You what?" She looked around. "Why? I thought you were taking me hom- I wanted to go ..." she grabbed her purse, mumbling about deep pockets and small phones.

I walked around the car and opened the door. "Ivy."

She ignored me, mashing buttons on her cell and grumbling about service on the island.

I shook my head and wrapped my hand around her upper arm, tugging gently. "Come on, we need to talk and –"

She jerked away from me and glared. "We've talked enough! I just wanted to go *home*." She whined the last word as she gave up and tossed her phone back into her bag. "Stupid phone, stubborn man, ... I ... want ..., nightmare to end ...",

Her words jumbled and deteriorated into a sob. I leaned over and pulled her now unresisting body from the car. "Come on, you could use a drink."

I led her up the oyster shell sidewalk and in seconds we were standing in the living room of my small cottage. I guided her to the sofa and then headed to the kitchen, filling two glasses with ice, and grabbing a half bottle of whisky.

I returned to the living room to find Ivy standing with her arms wrapped tightly around herself sniffling and staring out through the sliding glass doors. Grateful the tears seemed to have stopped, I poured us each a shot and contemplated the best way to approach the questioning; the last thing I wanted was her in hysterics.

"Here, drink this."

She stared at me and then accepted the glass, downing the shot in one gulp before handing it back with a silent nod for another.

My eyebrows rose and I bit back a laugh before splashing a thimbleful over the ice. I set the bottle on the coffee table. "Go easy, baby. I want you calm, not comatose."

Her eyes went wide and her hand shook. "You want ..." she dropped the glass and backed away, coming to a stop when she reached the door.

I frowned at her reaction and then it dawned on me. I laughed and reached for her, then thought better of it and moved to sit on the sofa. "Calm down Ivy, I'm not going to hurt you."

I chuckled and shook my head. "I brought you here to keep you from getting hurt," I smirked. "Well, and to get some answers but, the main goal tonight is keeping you from harm," I patted the sofa. "Have a seat and try to relax."

Some of the tension left her shoulders but she made no move to sit beside me. "What do you mean, keep me from getting hurt? Who would want to hurt me?" She waved her hand. "I mean, apart from the mugger, and that was just random."

My eyebrows rose. "Think so? Think every small-time hoodlum in Savannah walks up to people with a knife and demands only the ring they're wearing?" I again patted the seat. "Or how about burglars. What are the statistics for B & E in the metro where no property is taken?"

Her mouth dropped open and then closed with a snap. I could see the wheels turning, she was naïve but not stupid, and as the shock wore off, she was putting the pieces together. It only remained to be seen if she'd accept the reality of her situation.

She swallowed several times and then sighed, turning back towards the door. Arms wrapped tightly around herself and head bowed, she looked forlorn and just a little lost.

Despite my better instincts, I set my drink down and moved to stand behind her. When she made no move to distance herself, I eased closer and enveloped her in my arms.

She stiffened for a moment before sighing and almost wilting. A muffled sob escaped her. "Why is this all happening to me? I'm beginning to think I'm cursed."

I sighed, wondering how much to say. I knew why, at least part of the why, and it had nothing to do with curses unless you considered James Brogan a curse.

I toyed with the idea of telling her about the ring and had it on the tip of my tongue, but before I could speak, Ivy turned and pressed herself to my chest. She raised her face, her silent plea unmistakable.

I groaned and my gaze fastened on her slightly parted and moist lips. Branding myself a fool, I surrendered to her invitation.

Cards on the Table

Ivy

I stirred and eased myself out from under Dom's arm. Careful not to wake him, I stood and gathered my clothes and then searched for a bathroom. I dressed, splashed water on my face, and squeezed some toothpaste on my finger, brushing my teeth as best I could before taking a hard look at myself in the mirror. No amount of water or toothpaste was going to help how I felt inside.

I stepped out of the bathroom and tiptoed back to the living room, dreading Dom's waking. The last thing

I wanted to do at the moment was make awkward small talk. What did one say after a quickie with a first date? Thanks for the booty call; see ya on the flip side?

Recriminations slammed me from all sides. Climbing into bed with a guy I'd just met, God! Maybe easy virtue ran in my genes. I shook my head and tried to console myself with the excuse that I'd been in shock, that it'd been a heck of a month, that I'd been half-drunk, but truth was, I'd just felt like it.

Felt like throwing all of my cautions to the wind and taking what I wanted, to hell with consequences, with propriety, with rational thought; I'd just wanted to feel and be. I cringed, cursing myself for being every kind of a fool, and steeled myself for a morning after dance. A glance at Dom showed he was still fast asleep.

I sighed, grateful for the reprieve, and flipped the latch on the sliding glass door. A cool ocean breeze whipped my hair and goose flesh pricked my arms. I turned and snagged a blanket off the back of a chair and then pulled the door shut. Drawing a deep breath of salty air, I headed for the wooden walkway that ran across the dunes.

Seagulls cawed overhead, circling and diving toward the washed-up crabs littering the surf line. The tide was on its way in, and waves slammed the shore one after another, the roar competing with the voice of my conscience screaming in my head.

I pulled the thin blanket closer to my neck and headed for a dry spot in the sand beside a deep tidal pool. I nestled in the cool sand, scrunched my toes deep beneath it, and tried to rationalize last night's behavior.

Try as I might, there was no good excuse. I'd been upset, but who wouldn't be after facing a potential mugger? That didn't make what I'd done any more tolerable. Oh, why didn't I listen to that inner voice, the one that screamed at me to stop last night?

The answer was simple. I'd given in to lust and allowed myself to be charmed by his attentiveness and wit. Powerful memories of last night rose in my mind.

I drew a deep, steadying breath. Dominic Riordan was dangerous to my peace of mind. I had no doubt he was a great guy, certainly the best I'd ever met or dated, but disgust still roiled within me.

For years, I'd been a silent witness to the many 'uncles' Aunt Fey had hooked up with. Each one had left his mark on younger me. The new-age guru hadn't been all bad, at least he'd paid my tuition to a private school, but there had always been a price and a reckoning. The fake shaman had proved that.

I squirmed, remembering the night "Uncle" Lone Wolf decided my adolescent body should be initiated into his brand of spiritual awareness. I shuddered to think what might have happened had Aunt Fey not returned early from her job and knocked him out cold with a ceremonial Indian totem.

That had been the end of our sojourn on an Indian reservation and the end of my innocence. From that day forward, I'd viewed each of my aunt's 'friends' with a jaundiced eye and heavy suspicion.

If I was honest with myself, those views had transferred to every man I met-until now. Dominic Riordan was different, though I couldn't say exactly why. He was handsome, but that wasn't what drew me. I'd learned last night that he knew what it felt like to lose a parent at an early age.

He hadn't lived on the road, but he did understand the loneliness and longing for a stable home. I'd sensed it in his voice when he spoke of his father and the shrimp business.

He hadn't talked about it, but I suspected the long days out on the ocean, away from civilization had set him apart from his peers, and bothered him in much the same way as what I had experienced.

I sighed and rested my chin on my raised knees. Perhaps that was why I trusted him. Oh, there had been a few moments when my default suspicion of all men had reared its head, but on an instinctive level, I connected with him, we shared common ground.

I felt safe with him ... I frowned, recalling Dom's insistence that he'd brought me to his home for my safety.

My instinct was to dismiss it, he was just making excuses to get into my- I rolled my eyes and pushed that line of thought away, I'd given him that without a whimper- no more self-recriminations.

I shook my head and let a handful of sand sift through my fingers. The tiny grains sparkled in the early morning sun, blending with the blue light cast from the ring on my finger. I raised my hand in front of my face and stared at the large, square stone.

Why had that man only demanded the ring? I'd like to think he was just interrupted before he could demand our wallets or other items, but logic wouldn't allow it; it'd been dark and my hand was partially up my sleeve, the mugger wouldn't have even known I was wearing a ring.

It was costume jewelry, or so I'd thought, but a man had risked jail time for it, and then there was the break-in ...

Was Dom, right? Were they connected events? But why? How would anyone know I had-

"Ivy?"

I whipped around to see Dom approaching. Low-slung jeans clung to lean hips and an open shirt framed an envy-producing six-pack, he was a good-looking man! I pushed aside my lusty inner self and forced myself to stay focused.

Dom sank down beside me and leaned in, kissing me on the cheek. "Good morning, are you always such an early riser?"

I blinked. So much for morning-after awkwardness. The brief thought that he did this often reared its head, but my non-jealous side reminded me that he'd had to go search for a condom so ...

Striving for a light, unaffected tone, I laughed. "Um, it's not that early. About seven-thirty."

He chuckled and put an arm around me, under the blanket. "That's pretty early to me, after last night's excitement anyway."

"About that ..." Deciding to ignore what he'd obviously meant by excitement; I steered the conversation to safer waters, and wasn't that just ironic?

I held up my hand, letting the blue-stoned ring catch the light. "Do you think someone is trying to steal this ring from me?"

Dom stiffened and drew away. "Well, uh ..." he scratched at the stubble on his cheek. "It seems possible. What do you think?"

I frowned. Last night he'd been adamant- no *mocking* of me for not seeing what he clearly thought was obvious and now he seemed to be backing away from that assessment.

I leaned back, the better to view his expressions as I pushed. "You're the ex-cop and now security expert, you tell me."

As I'd sensed, he was uncomfortable but trying to hide it.

"Um, that's true." He laughed, though it sounded forced. "How about we get some breakfast, at least some coffee ..." he stood and held out a hand. "We can discuss it after caffeine."

I stared, long enough to make him fidget, and then relented, taking his offer of assistance to help me to my feet. "Sounds good." I brushed the sand off of my backside and drew the blanket closed before striding towards the boardwalk, tossing over my shoulder, "But after coffee, you can tell me what you know about this ring."

I smirked as his mouth dropped open. Good. About time I was in control of what was turning out to be a wild ride.

Dom

I stirred a teaspoon of sugar into my cup and searched for words. After throwing me off balance on the beach, she'd let it all simmer long enough for some toast and coffee, but now, the second cup in front of me, Ivy wanted answers.

She leaned her hip against the breakfast bar, arms folded across herself. "So, tell me what you know about my Aunt Fey and her jewelry."

I sipped the hot liquid and measured my response. "Well, I don't know anything about your aunt or *her* jewelry ..." I nodded towards her finger, "but I do know that ring isn't hers."

I cleared my throat and schooled my features to as near to neutral as I could manage. "The first time I saw that blue diamond was in my mother's hand the night she was murdered."

Ivy gasped and my gaze whipped toward her.

"You ... there's some kind of mistake." She gulped and waved her hand. "You're mistaken ... you have to be."

She frowned when I shook my head in the negative. Her face lost all color and I moved closer, wondering if she'd faint. "Maybe you should sit down ..."

She shook her head and waved away my concern. "Dom, I found this," she raised her hand. "I found this with my aunt's things. How can it be your mother's?"

I sighed and reached for her hand, staring at the ring. "There's no mistake, Ivy. I knew it the minute I saw you wearing it at the café. That is the ring I saw on my mother's hand just before she left our apartment for the last time."

Ivy stared at me and then down at her now trembling hand. She gulped several times, and it was clear she was processing what I'd told her. Several expressions crossed her face, but she shocked me when she jerked her hand away.

"Let me get this straight." Her voice was shaky, but the tone was hard as she continued. "You *think* this is a valuable ring, not a piece of costume jewelry." She shook her head. "And you think it is the same ring you saw your mother with the night she was killed."

I nodded. "Ivy, I don't think it, I know it." I pointed at her ring finger. "That ring is not glass. It is an antique blue diamond, and it was stolen almost twenty years ago."

"Why ..." She cleared her throat. "I mean, if you suspected this ring belonged to your mother from the beginning, why didn't you say something then?"

I started to make an excuse when her eyes opened wide, and her voice raised an octave. "Wait a minute! Was that why you looked so sick when we met?"

I sighed and looked away from her piercing stare. Part of me wanted to just tell everything I knew and let the chips fall, but I also worried that she'd tip my hand to Brogan. I was not nearly as confident as I wanted to be regarding her relationship with her godfather.

"Well? What is the deal? How do you think this is the same ring and, if it is, why did my Aunt Fey have it?"

Her tone was aggressive and just a bit mocking. It pushed my temper. I slammed my mug down onto the counter and snarled. "Look, I know that is the ring my mother was wearing the night she died. I've been searching for it for almost twenty years, so yeah, seeing it on your hand tipped me for a loop and yes, I am very sure that is the same ring!"

Ivy frowned. "You've been searching ... why?" What is the big deal about this ring? And why didn't you say something the minute you saw it?"

I dragged a hand through my hair and glanced at her before staring out at the ocean, trying to rein in my anger. When I felt controlled, I chose my words carefully. "I've been searching for it because I believe it is why she was murdered."

A harshly drawn breath from me made me turn. Her anger was cooling, replaced with what I thought looked like pity. My stomach tightened at the thought, but I'd take it over anger. Empathy I could work with.

She closed the space between us and hesitantly put her arms around my waist. "I'm so sorry." She looked up at me, her blue eyes welling with tears, and I felt gratitude for her caring but also guilty because I wasn't above using her nature against her. I closed my eyes.

God, what a mess. Why couldn't she have been an unattractive, man-hating, she-devil? Why did the girl of my dreams have to be tied to the nightmare of my life?

My conscious was screaming to let go and trust her with all of my suspicions. That if I didn't, I'd wreck all chances of a future with her. Did I risk blowing the one shot I had at solving the mystery that had haunted me for years in the hopes of a relationship with Ivy?

"Why didn't you tell me this right away? Why wait until now?"

I drew a deep breath and decided to take a chance on the flame-haired siren that was Ivy Michaels. "I ..." my voice cracked, and I swallowed past the lump in my throat. "I had to make sure you weren't involved first."

Ivy stiffened in my arms and jerked away. Her mouth was hanging open and her eyes were wide. She gaped several times as if searching for words.

I frowned. Not the reaction I'd been expecting. "Ivy? Uh, what- "

"How dare you?" She glared and then whipped around, rummaging under the throw blanket on the couch, and then got down onto her knees, searching under the coffee table as she muttered, "where is the darn – "

I joined her in the living area. "Ivy? What are you ... what is going on?"

She looked up and scowled. "What is – are you serious?" She turned her attention back to the floor and wriggled on her stomach, reaching with her arm. "Ah, there you are!"

She emerged from under the table, cell phone in hand. She mashed several buttons and then looked at me, hands on her hips. "What's all this been then ... your special brand of inquisition?" She rolled her eyes, muttering under her breath.

"Ivy, I don't understand. What are you so angry about?" I shook my head, trying to recall what I'd said that would have sent her into orbit.

I'd told her I'd had to make sure she wasn't involved in the case surrounding the ring but why would that ... I scratched my head.

She stopped midway towards the front door, turning to glare at him. "Why am I angry?"

I winced as her voice rose towards the range only dogs would hear. I held out my hands in supplication. Protection? I had no idea, still wondering just how the situation had escalated to a fight. A near growl drew my attention.

"Do you sleep with all the female suspects you believe are thieves or possible murderers?"

"What? I didn't accuse you- "

"Huh! Did you or did you not just say you kept your suspicions about this ring to yourself because you weren't sure I wasn't involved in some criminal activity?"

I huffed. "I'm not saying you are a thief and don't blame me for the sex, you were more than willing!"

I grimaced and wished I could hit rewind as Ivy's face went white and then a mottled shade of red.

"Bastard." Her shoulders drooped and her anger seemed to dissolve as quickly as it'd risen. "Once again, my ability to attract rat bastard men is confirmed." She shook her head and moved to the front door, leaning against the jam as she looked out the side window.

I sighed and wondered just how I'd managed to so royally screw up in such a short period. "Ivy ..." I dragged a hand through my hair. "Look, I never thought you were the one that stole the ring, and I certainly never thought you were a party to murder!"

She glanced over her shoulder, a smirk twisting her lovely lips. "Then just what part did you think I was playing?"

I took a step closer, thought better of it, and leaned against the breakfast bar. Arms folded across my chest, I stared at her for several minutes, debating my answer. Tired of the sparring and figuring I was damned either way, I decided on the truth, the whole truth, so help me ...

I drew a deep breath. "Look, right or wrong, the first time I saw you, you were kissing James Brogan and wearing that ring. What was I supposed to think?"

Her head whipped around. "Wha- kissing James ... he's, my godfather! What does that have to do with anything?" She shook her head. "You know what? Just forget it. You make no sense." She scoffed. "Some detective you are, no wonder you're no longer on the force!"

My hands clenched into fists and an ugly stream of curses fell from my lips. I stepped away from the bar and then stopped as I caught sight of Ivy's face.

"Oh, for God's sake, wipe that fear off your face. I'm not going to hurt you!"

Her eyebrows rose. "Could have fooled me. You look madder than a hornet."

I closed my eyes and drew a deep breath. When I finally met her eyes, I felt back in control. "Look, Ivy, I can explain everything, and I have proof, sort of, just come sit down and I'll- "

"Just tell me now." She looked down at her phone. "And make it quick, my ride will be here in about five minutes."

I gritted my teeth and opened my mouth to argue but a car horn sounded in the drive, and I knew if I didn't tell her now, I'd never get the chance.

I held out my hand. "All right, just ... I need a few minutes."

She tapped on her phone and then nodded. "Five minutes, start talking."

I rolled my eyes but refrained from wasting my allotted time with more arguing. "Fine, you want the truth, here it is." I started pacing as the facts filled my mind. "According to my investigation, that blue diamond you're wearing was reported stolen in 1999. Guess who owned it?"

I smirked at her but didn't give her a chance to respond. "That's right, you're precious godfather, James Brogan. He owned it and reported it stolen. Got a boatload of insurance money for it, from what I can gather."

She started to speak but I held up my hand and pushed on. "Then a few years later, it resurfaced in my mom's hand. A couple hours after I saw her with it, she turned up dead by the Waving Girl statue on River Street."

I glared at her. "Now, you want to tell me how the thing ended up with your aunt? I don't know but I intend to find out!"

Ivy frowned. "I'm sorry about your mom, but Dom, nothing you've said makes any sense. I mean, so Jamie owned the ring. It was stolen and then whoever did that sold it or something and somehow your mom got it."

She shook her head. "You drag my godfather into this and now my aunt, but it's just ..." she huffed and opened the door. "Since you're such a great private *dick*, did it ever occur to you that the person who stole it was responsible for your mom's murder or maybe she was involved with the thief? I mean, that makes a lot more sense."

I sucked in a breath as Ivy flung her pronouncement at me and then stalked out the front door. I gulped and recovered enough to chase after her. "My mother wasn't perfect,"

Ivy stopped and turned. "Look, I shouldn't have been so ... bitchy about it. I'm sorry for your loss but you're grasping at straws, and I'm done so ..."

She started walking towards the car parked in my drive. "Ivy, I know she wasn't involved with the theft. I haven't figured out how she got the ring yet, but I will, and when I do, James Brogan is going down for insurance fraud and murder."

She crossed in front of the idling car, not even bothering to respond.

I raised my voice. "I'll tell you something else, babe. Brogan is responsible for all the stuff happening to you lately."

That got her attention. She looked at me over the top of the car, leaned in to say something to the girl driving, then looked back at him. "You're obsessed. You should get help."

I shook my head. "Think about it, Ivy. Why else would someone break into your place, rummage around and not take anything? Then there's our little attacker last night that only asked for your ring. He set it all up, I feel it in my bones."

Ivy laughed. "God, you have issues dude, get some help. You hate Jamie, though I don't know why, and your perspective is skewed."

She got into the car and I rushed forward, leaning down to speak through the driver's opened window. "You want to know why I hate James Brogan? He's the reason I'm no longer a detective. My investigation into my mother's murder led me to the ring and ultimately to him."

I ignored the gasp from the driver, holding Ivy's gaze. "I don't know how he and my mom were involved but I do know there was suspicion about the ring's theft. The investigation was called off and I suspect it was

Brogan using his influence, just as he did when I started asking questions." I sighed, "Look, Ivy, trust me, the guy is knee-deep in this crap and-"

Ivy laughed. "Trust you? That's rich!" she waved a hand of dismissal and turned to her friend. "Come on Tina, breakfast is on me."

I jumped back as the car peeled out of the drive. I blew out a breath. That could have gone better. I rolled my eyes and stalked back to the house.

I'd handled everything wrong. She hadn't believed a word I'd said about Brogan, and it was highly doubtful she accepted my belief that she was in danger.

I slammed my hand down onto the bar and wondered if I could have screwed up any better if I'd tried.

On top of getting nowhere with my investigation, I had probably ruined all chances of a relationship with Ivy. The fact that I was more upset about that than a stymied case made me grit my teeth.

I needed emotional involvement like I needed another hole in my head, but I couldn't lie, I was attracted to Ivy, probably more so now that I'd had a dose of her temper.

I huffed and poured another cup of coffee. What did that say about me? Better yet, what was drawing me to the little witch with the sharp tongue? I'd dated lots of women, taken a few to bed, and even come close to proposing once before my career took a nosedive.

Pride had stopped me then. What could a disgraced and out-of-work cop offer? A year later, the bitterness of my dismissal behind me and a new company taking off, I'd sighed and sent a silent thank you skyward that forces beyond my control had kept me from biting that bullet.

Looking back, I could admit that more than pride had stopped me from marrying. The women I'd been involved with were all career-oriented, most to the point of obsession. Perhaps my subconscious had realized none of them was the type to put husband and children first, which brought me back to Ivy.

She longed for a home and family. I could relate. Her unorthodox childhood made her want nothing so much as stability. Her down-to-earth demeanor and lifestyle suggested she'd have a passel of kids someday and be at every soccer game and PTO meeting.

I liked that. I wanted that for my kids. God only knew I didn't want to inflict a self-absorbed, flighty woman like my mother onto any child.

I shook my head. Where had that come from? I shoved the crazy thoughts aside. What was I thinking? I'd just met the woman, and given the last couple of hours, she'd probably choose to chew nails rather than talk to me. I was getting old.

I scratched at the stubble on my chin. Marriage and kids. That was the last thing Ivy Michaels would be thinking where I was concerned.

I stiffened as a thought struck me. As angry as she was, she'd probably refuse the security system. She'd be a sitting duck, especially since she refused to believe my suspicions about Brogan.

I grabbed my cell and called the office. A quick chat with my secretary and I let out a pent-up breath. My techs were already at work installing the alarms so that decision was taken out of her hands. I could only hope it was enough to keep her safe until she came to her senses and put her trust in me.

Denial is a River

Ivy

The thrum of tuning instruments and mic checks blended with the familiar kitchen noises of banging pots and running water.

"Testing, one, two ... testing."

I set the last appetizer onto the buffet table and turned to take it all in. My gaze wandered over the small stage where Thomas and his band were assembling, then on toward the front windows where a blue neon sign now proclaimed that the Cosmic Café was open for business.

I smiled and watched my wait staff head to the kitchen for last-minute instructions. In less than an hour, the doors would open, the band would rock, and hopefully, the money would roll.

It was hard to believe my dream was coming to fruition. I felt like asking Tina for a pinch, just to see if everything was real. I'd worked hard for this moment and the only thing that would have made me happier was if Aunt Fey were there to share it; and, I had to admit, Dom Riordan.

I'd ranted the whole way home from Tybee, poor Tina just nodding and making sympathetic noises about unreliable men, many fishes, and getting back onto the horse, until I had made the mistake of telling her about Dom's mother, his beliefs about the blue diamond, and James Brogan.

Tina had surprised me by taking Dom's side and when we pulled up to the townhouse and saw his techs were just finishing the install, Tina went into full-on head cheerleader for Team Riordan.

"Look, Ivy. I think you should at least give him another chance."

I rolled my eyes and continued to inspect the security system, paying particular attention to the tech as he explained the panic button on the keypad located in her bedroom and another by my front door.

I signed the work order and then turned to see what good fortune had stopped Tina harassing me about

Dom. I grinned and silently thanked my fluffy white beggar as Tina bent to offer him another kitty treat.

"Don't give him too many, he's already a pudge ball."

Tina laughed and set the bag on a high shelf. "If I feed him, he doesn't bite me."

I smirked and moved the bag of treats back to the cupboard, no sense enticing Sergeant to climb. "News flash, he will bite the hand that feeds him given the slightest provocation."

Tina grinned and nodded. "Oh, I know," she scratched behind the feline in question's ears and then joined me in the kitchen. "I've seen the band-aids on your hands. He's a grumpy fluff ball, no doubt."

I opened my mouth to agree but stopped when Tina held up her hand and rushed on. "No, don't try and distract me, we are going to discuss this murder stuff and the great guy that is trying to keep you safe."

I scowled. "Great guy? You haven't met him! And have you heard nothing I've said? He screwed me for info!"

Tina rolled her eyes. "Don't be so dramatic! From what you said that part was mutual and just possibly a little more your fault than his-no, don't shoot me, I'm just going by your own words and being impartial!"

I sighed and shoved a mug of herbal tea across the counter to my friend before carrying my own to the little glass bistro set that afforded views of the courtyard below. "You're right." I nodded as Tina sat down. "In my defense, I was definitely in shock or something."

Tina shook her head. "Why does it have to be anything like that? You're an adult, single, you used protection. Just let it go at what it was or better yet, don't stand in the way of what it could yet be."

"Oh right, we had a nasty bit of verbal fighting, and you think we are headed towards couple of the year."

"No, I think any man that lets you flay him with your wickedly sharp tongue and still makes sure your security system is up and running at the crack of dawn is one to at least give a second chance to."

I stared down at the small oasis of green just coming to life for the season and struggled to admit that Tina had a point, which led me right back to what Dom had revealed about the ring and all the baggage that went with it. I raised my hand and nodded toward Tina.

"So, you think he could be right about this thing? That somehow my aunt, whose apartment you saw, could have owned a really valuable piece of jewelry and that it was involved in some kind of crime?"

Tina bit her lip, looked out the window, then back at me. She winced and then nodded. "Look, don't eat me, okay?"

I nodded and steeled myself for what my blunt friend might say.

"You've told me that your Aunt Fey was ... well-"

"Free-spirited is the kindest way to describe her."

Tina grinned. "Yes! That's what you always say, free-spirited and I've heard you add, free-loving."

I frowned but nodded in agreement. I usually did put those two descriptors together.

"So, because you know that your aunt dated lots of men and because you know from experience, she didn't always have the best taste ..."

I pursed my lips and thought about where Tina was going. It did ring true. "You're suggesting it isn't beyond the realm of possibility that Aunt Fey got the ring from a man she was involved with."

Tina nodded. "Yeah, I mean, everything Dom told you about the ring could be true, but it doesn't have to follow that Aunt Fey was the guilty one. She could have come by it honestly, right?"

"Yes, you're right! Which means, what?" I looked down at the ring, turning my hand to watch as the light bounced off of the stone. Could it be real?

It was certainly clearer than any fake diamond I'd ever seen, and the color was flawless, an endless sea of bright blue. Still, the idea was preposterous. My aunt was not the type to own anything that valuable, and while her lifestyle was unconventional, she was no thief.

But my gut said that no glass had ever shined like that and admitting that, I then had to accept what Dom Riordan believed could be true.

I met Tina's gaze and shrugged. "So, what do I do?"

Tina smiled. "Call him, Chickee."

I rolled my eyes. "And say what? I'm sorry I said lots of snarky things to you, want to come over for a roll in the hay?"

Tina laughed. "Well, that's what I would do but I doubt you can pull it off."

I scowled but knew my friend was right. "Not helping ..."

Tina rose and carried her mug to the sink. "Sorry. So, how about calling and thanking him for the quick install?" She rinsed her cup and placed it into the dishwasher before turning to face me.

"I ..., well I do need to pay him so ..."

Tina leaned against the sink and crossed her arms. "You can call the office for that. You need to call him directly."

I wrinkled my nose, not at all comfortable with the idea of calling and groveling, which I had no trouble admitting.

"Why is it groveling?" Tina shook her head. "It's not like you to avoid the hard stuff, that's more my thing. So why are you afraid to call him and apologize?"

I joined Tina at the sink, putting my mug away and tidying the counter before replying. "Maybe because I'm not sorry." I walked toward the bedroom, knowing Tina would follow. "I mean, I'm sorry we ended on a bad note, before the stupid mugger stuff I'd had a great time."

"So, just go with that!"

Tina sat on the bed as I grabbed some clothes from the dresser. I carried everything into the bathroom and turned on the water, raising my voice as I began to shower. "And just ignore everything that happened after? I don't think you get a dating mulligan."

Tina's laugh echoed as she moved to stand in the open doorway. "Wish there was such a thing! But seriously, just call and say ... I don't know ... that you are happy with the install and that you've been thinking about all that he's said and maybe there is something to it so you're glad for the system."

I had gotten ready for the day and rode to the café with Tina, pondering all that had been suggested but, in the end, I had not found the courage to call, merely paying the bill through the secretary.

I looked to the back of the café, watching as Tina talked with the staff, and wondered at my friend's apparent lack of further interest in my love life. We'd both been busy over the last few days, but it was still surprising that Tina had said very little to me about Dom or bugged me about whether I'd called him.

I walked behind the bar and checked the coffee station, the ice well, and liquor supplies. Everything was set. I shook my head and pushed aside my worries and unresolved potential love life. This was my night, and I wouldn't let anything quell my enjoyment of it.

A knock at the door drew my gaze. I frowned as I recognized the two detectives investigating my aunt's murder. My shoulders sagged, so much for nothing ruining my night.

I pasted a smile on my face and pushed the door open. "Hello, detectives."

"Ma'am." The older man nodded. "Sorry to bother you but we need to ask a few more questions."

I glanced over my shoulder and saw that the band had finished their preparations and were now heading toward the buffet. Laughter echoed from the rear of the house, but the dining room was empty. "Of course, anything I can do to help but can you make it fast? This is my opening night."

The two men nodded and followed me to a corner table. They refused my offer of drinks and I slid into a chair. "So, how can I help you?"

The men exchanged a glance before the older of the two spoke. "We ran your aunt's name and found she was wanted for questioning involving a crime committed in 2002."

I swallowed hard and strained to keep the shock from my face. "Aunt Fey? What ... how was she involved in a crime?"

Detective Hallowell cocked his head. His gaze searched my face. "We don't think she was, ma'am, but she was living with a man who was a suspect in an ongoing investigation."

I bit my lip and thought of all the things Dom had said about the ring and my aunt. "I see. What uh, ... what kind of crime?"

The younger detective leaned forward. "The murder of socialite Lorena Riordan."

I gasped and tried to calm my now racing heart as puzzle pieces clicked into place. I swallowed hard and attempted to keep my voice steady. "I ... you think Aunt Fey knew something about this?"

Detective Adkins raised an eyebrow. "We were hoping you could tell us."

I looked down at the table as my thoughts raced. Should I show them the ring and tell them how Dom thought they were connected? My first thought was yes, dump everything I knew into the detectives' laps and get on with my life, but my heart said wait, wait and tell Dom; It was his case, his mother.

My heart won. "Um, offhand I can't tell you anything. I was only about nine years old then." I looked up and found Detective Adkins staring at me. "I don't understand. If you know who committed this crime, why aren't you looking for him, why-"

"Frank Nolan is dead. He was found shot to death the day before your aunt left Savannah."

My eyes went wide and a soft "Oh!" escaped my lips.

The detective narrowed his eyes. "Did your aunt ever mention a boyfriend?"

I shook my head. "No, Aunt Fey didn't believe in looking back. She always said, if you retrace your footsteps, you're bound to fall in."

A sneer curled the young detective's lips. "Convenient."

I clamped my lips together and silently counted to ten. I didn't like the guy's attitude but getting into a verbal war with him would only prolong the interview. I didn't need that right now.

Detective Hallowell cleared his throat, drawing my gaze. The older man offered an apologetic smile. "We understand you were just a child, ma'am. Our investigation shows that Ms. Michaels cleared out her bank account and left town two days after the murder. Sources revealed she had a young girl with her. Can you tell us anything about that?"

I drew a deep breath. "Well, I was the child with her, but I don't know why we left Savannah." Detective Adkins scowled. "Your aunt takes off with you and you don't know why?"

Irritated by his tone, I addressed my remarks to the older man. "My parents were killed in a car accident about a month before we left Savannah. Aunt Fey just said we needed a fresh start and an adventure to take our minds off things." I met his gaze, willing him to understand. "I was nine and grieving; I didn't ask many questions."

Detective Hallowell smiled at me and nodded. "We understand, Miss Michaels. Could you tell us what you do remember about your last days in Savannah?"

I checked my watch, two hours until opening. I bit my lip and debated telling them to come back later but everything was done, and I wanted it all to end so I nodded and briefly told them about Fey waking me with an order to pack. I touched on our visit to the lawyer's office and hopping on the train to Florida, but I excluded the bank stop and didn't offer any information about the safety deposit box or its contents.

Guilt flashed in my mind, but I suppressed it. Too many coincidences were stacking up. Too many questions remained unanswered. The possibility of the police department being less than discreet made me uncomfortable with revealing the contents of the bank box. Dom's accusations against my godfather rang in my ears.

I pushed it to the back of my mind because the trail wasn't leading to Jamie, but to my aunt. I hated to admit it, but I owed it to Dom to tell him first.

I decided a little digging was in order before I turned everything over to the authorities, too. If anyone was going to muck through my aunt's past, and possibly unearth skeletons, it would be me. I owed Aunt Fey that much.

"I'm sorry I can't be of more help, detectives."

"That's all right; we appreciate your time." I winced as Detective Hallowell patted my hand and mashed the ring into my skin. "Oh, sorry. Did I hurt you?"

I shook my head. "It's all right; don't worry about it." Detective Hallowell shrugged. "Pretty ring ya got there."

I smiled but refused to comment. I hoped my face showed none of my inner alarm as I surreptitiously tucked my hand into my lap.

Detective Adkins' gaze followed my movements. I bristled under the younger man's stare. He stared at me for several seconds before continuing with his questions. "When you went through your aunt's things, did you happen to find anything unusual?"

My heart started to thump in her chest. I gulped and tried to remain cool. "Unusual? I'm not sure what you mean. My aunt didn't have much. Just some old books and clothes. Oh, and I found a sketch pad full of drawings."

Detective Adkins' eyes narrowed. "Was there anything else?"

I flashed them a smile and rose from the table, signaling the interview to be at an end. "No, I told you she didn't have much. Now, if you'll excuse me ..." I stood and offered my hand. "Sorry I couldn't be of more help."

Detective Hallowell pumped my hand and smiled, assuring me that every bit of information helped but his partner gave me a hard stare that made me squirm. I flashed my brightest smile and turned away to speak to the older man. "Detective Hallowell? Could you, that is, I was wondering if the coroner determined the cause of death for my aunt?"

"Yes, he did. I thought they told you when you claimed the- no matter, just keep it to yourself, all right Miss? We're not releasing some of the details."

I nodded. "Of course, I understand and, if you'd rather not say, that's okay. I probably don't want to know."

He shook his head and headed towards the door. "Sometimes it helps to know, Miss. Eases the pain of wondering and all. The vict- I mean your aunt was strangled. No signs of sexual assault, no signs of robbery."

I gulped and wished I hadn't asked. "Ah, thanks ... that is," I cleared my throat. "That is a relief of sorts." I shivered and wrapped my arms around myself, watching as they left the café.

Ivy

Music rocked through the café, mingling with the chatter of patrons. The Cosmic Café's opening could only be dubbed a rousing success. Every table was taken, and my wait staff was handling the crowd with aplomb.

I slipped out from behind the bar and wove my way through the tables, stopping to greet friends and introduce myself to strangers. My heart swelled with pride. My dream was off to a great start, and from the compliments, I'd received, it looked like many here tonight would soon be regulars.

"Ivy!"

I looked around the crowded room and then smiled as I found my godfather's table. I'd seen him and his guests in the bar earlier but hadn't had a chance to chat. I headed toward his corner table.

"Ivy." James Brogan rose and enfolded me in an exuberant hug. He wrapped an arm around my waist, kissed my cheek, and then turned back to his guests. "Your attention, please. Join me in congratulating my goddaughter, the owner of the Cosmic Café, Ivy Michaels."

My cheeks burned as the group clapped and offered praise for the café, the band, and the food. I waved away their applause with a smile. "Thank you! I'm so happy that everything meets with your approval, and I hope you'll make the Cosmic Café a regular dining exper- "

"Wow!" A well-dressed older woman at the table interrupted. "That is some rock. Looks like someone has a very generous boyfriend!"

I struggled to maintain an unconcerned façade as the rest of the table laughed at the lady's jest. I felt Jaime stiffen and Dom's suspicions about the origins of the ring came rushing back. I mentally cursed myself for not removing it, then opened my mouth to brush away the comment. I swallowed my retort as my godfather spoke first.

"That thing? Gabby, you must be losing your touch; it looks like a bit of colored glass to me." Brogan flashed me an apologetic smile as everyone chuckled. "Sorry darlin', I don't mean to be insulting." He squeezed me then slid back onto his chair. "If I know Ivy, she picked up that bit of costume jewelry at one of those secondhand shops she loves so much."

Everyone laughed and the conversation turned to the upcoming Saint Patrick's Day events and whether my godfather's appearance in the parade would help his congressional campaign. I forced a smile and took my to leave, making the excuse that I had a million things to do.

I couldn't focus on anything but Jaime's reaction and comment concerning the ring. I looked back toward the table and gasped as my eyes locked with his. For just a second, his expression was unguarded, and the look directed at me was cold, calculating, and full of rage.

I gulped and averted my gaze, fighting back the bile rising in my throat as fear crept along my spine. For the first time, I considered the possibility that my godfather was involved in the crimes Dom attributed to him.

I pushed the thought away and glanced back to see Jaime smiling at me, face relaxed and eyes twinkling. I flashed a quick smile back and then went to the server station to tally receipts. I shook my head at my foolishness.

I'd been imagining things; my godfather was the reason I had the Cosmic Café. He was always there for me, and I felt guilty even entertaining the notion that he could be involved in the things Dom suggested.

Still, I couldn't quite shake the feeling I'd gotten when Jamie had remarked on the ring. It had seemed as if he wanted to divert everyone's attention and change the subject.

A glance at the clock showed the band would be wrapping up in about ten minutes. I instructed the staff to begin closing procedures and then let my mind drift. I worried at my lower lip and stared at the cash register as it printed off the night's receipts.

Jaime had been more than good to me. He deserved my unwavering loyalty, yet the coincidences were mounting, and I was finding it more and more difficult to dismiss them.

I gritted my teeth. Dom and his allegations. My mind hadn't been easy since learning of his suspicions. Because of him, I was seeing conspiracies in every innocuous remark.

I pursed my lips. The sooner I got that man and his crazy theories out of my head, the better. I ripped off the receipt tape and gathered the cash from the till. Heading to the office, I turned and slammed nose-first into a solid wall of muscle.

"Whoa, careful Ivy." Strong hands gripped my shoulders, steadying me.

I looked up, ready to offer an apology and thanks but both died on my lips as I stared into Dom's familiar blue eyes.

"Speak of the devil." I jerked away from his hands and took a step back. "What are you doing here?"

Dom's eyebrows rose. "I came to wish you well." He frowned. "Wasn't aware I'd become the devil incarnate when the invitation was issued."

I scowled. "Invitation? We didn't- "

"I called him, Ivy."

I swung around to find Tina standing against the kitchen door.

"You what?"

She shrugged, a smile tugging at her lips. "You were never going to come off your high horse so ..." She nudged me aside and stuck her hand out toward Dom. "I'm Tina Crawford, Ivy's best friend, and kitchen manager."

"Not for much longer ..." I muttered under my breath.

"You love me." Tina stuck her tongue out and then winked at Dom. "You two play nice, I gotta finish shutting my kitchen down."

I scowled at Tina's back and then turned to Dom. I was painfully aware that the crowd was thinning, and we were conspicuous; my business did not need a scene in the dining room. I pasted a smile onto my face, but my tone remained flat.

"I appreciate you stopping by but we're getting ready to close. I have work to do, so if you'll excuse me ..."

I moved to step around him, but his hand wrapped around my upper arm, halting my progress. I gave him a withering glance and fought the nasty retort that sprang to my lips.

The look wasn't lost on him. He smirked but kept his hand on me. "I was worried about you tonight. Brogan's here and, well ..." He glanced down at the ring. "You're still wearing that."

I glared at him. "Of course I am! Why shouldn't I?"

Dom rolled his eyes. "You know why." He shook his head and muttered under his breath something about stubborn witches; at least I hoped that was what he'd said.

I pursed my lips and started to let another verbal arrow fly when Dom held up his hand. "Let's not fight, all right? I came because I care. How about I sit at the bar until you finish and then take you home?"

I frowned. A part of me was touched at his solicitude but my more cynical side reared its head to point out that he was just worried about solving his case and if anything happened to me ... I shook my head and jerked my arm away. "Are you insane? What makes you think I'd turn to you to keep me safe? For that matter, why should I even be concerned about safety?"

Dom's gaze shifted toward the corner table, his meaning obvious.

I huffed and stalked off toward the kitchen. Dom caught up with me just outside the swinging door. He grabbed my arm and tugged until I turned to face him.

"Okay, I get that you're still mad at me but be sensible, Ivy. You need protection, especially since you won't stay away from Brogan!" He nodded toward my hand. "You're so hard-headed you won't even take off the ring!" He gritted his teeth and raked a hand through his hair. "You need a keeper."

My eyes widened. "If my hands weren't full, I swear I'd slap you! I was just thinking about you and how your crazy theories have turned me into a paranoid nut. Because of you, I'm suspicious of everyone and I see goons lurking in every shadow!"

Dom smirked. "So, you've been thinking about me."

I rolled my eyes. "That's not a good thing, you ass!" I stiffened as I noticed several people looking our way. I took a deep breath and lowered my voice. "Look Dom,

I appreciate the thought but really, I can look out for myself. *If,* or when I choose to believe your wild accusations, I'll do some investigating. I've looked after myself for a long time and I'm neither stupid nor helpless- "

"*If* you accept my theories? How can you not after all that's happened to you?" He shook his head. "I never said you were stupid, Ivy, just stubborn, but the fact that Brogan is here proves you're not being careful."

I scowled. "What would you have me do? For crying out loud, Dom, he's my godfather and I can't just- "

"Ivy, is everything all right?"

Dom and I whirled around to see James Brogan behind us. Guilt over my suspicions reared its ugly head. I gulped and fervently hoped he hadn't heard our conversation. I laid my hand on Jamie's arm and saw Dom stiffen. I gave him a warning glance.

"Everything's fine, Jaime, my friend was just trying to convince me that I need an escort for the walk home. Are you guys getting ready to leave?"

Jamie's gaze was filled with contempt as he looked toward Dom, but his voice remained even as he answered me. "We had a wonderful dinner, Darlin' and everyone was pleased. You've earned some regular and loyal customers out of that crowd."

His gaze shifted to Dom. His tone never wavered from casual friendliness, but his eyes were cold and flat. "If you're worried about safety, Ivy, I'll send Rizzo back. He can drive you home." He looked at me, a tight smile on his lips. "I assure you that your trust is better placed with him than in a washed-out, disgraced cop."

My eyes widened and my mouth fell open. I stood in silence, my gaze darting from one man to the other as the tension mounted. They stood nose to nose, each glaring at the other with hate-filled eyes. In shock, I was unable to move or speak until I noticed Dom's hands clench into fists.

That propelled me into action. The last thing I needed was a brawl between an ex-cop and a congressional candidate on opening night. I stepped between the two men, forcing them to step back.

I scowled at Dom and then flashed my godfather a tight smile. "Jamie, I thank you for the offer, but I don't need anyone to escort me home. I'm a big girl-" Dom made a strangled noise and I rushed on, "and even if I did need a ride, I can get one from Tina so quit the pissing contest, okay?"

The corner of Jamie's lip twitched into a tell-tale smile. He glared at Dom, then nodded.

"You call me if you need me, Ivy." He dropped a light kiss onto my cheek before heading back to his guests.

I released my breath and thanked all benevolent gods I'd avoided making the morning news, although now that I thought about it ... I chuckled as I turned toward Dom, still hovering behind me

One glance showed he'd failed to see any humor in the situation. I rolled my eyes. "Just drop it." I blew a strand of hair out of my eyes, and it hit me that I was tired, dead tired. "Everything is fine. Just go home and let me take care of my business, *please*?"

Dom scowled. "If you think I'll be shooed off that easy, you're crazy!"

I sighed and rolled my shoulders. "Dom please, I don't need this right now. I get your concerns. I'll admit I have some myself and I'll get around to looking into things. In the meantime, I don't need you standing over my shoulder or picking fights with my customers!"

"He's not your customer; he's a murderer and a thief. Can't you get that through your head?"

I smirked and pushed the kitchen door open with my hip. "No, it's too thick, remember?"

I saw the color rise on his face and thought I might have pushed him too far. I braced myself for another round of sparring, but Dom must have realized I'd reached the end of my energy because all at once the tension left his body, and his features relaxed.

His lips twisted into a rueful smile. "Ivy ..." He chuckled and leaned towards me, pressing a butterfly soft kiss on my lips. "I just want you safe, angel. And as jeopardy friendly as you seem to be, that is a full-time job. Finish up here and let's talk, okay? I can wait at–"

133

"I've said all I'm going to on this subject tonight." I tried to ignore the awareness that was sizzling between us from that one gentle kiss. I swallowed, drew a shaky breath, and put some distance between us. "I ..., uh, I get that you are worried, and I'm grateful, really! But it's been a long day and I'm not through yet, so please, just leave."

He frowned and started to answer but I rushed on. "I'll call you if, and when, I find out anything. Does that make you feel better?"

His eyes narrowed. "Don't placate me, Ivy. And no, it doesn't. You do realize your godfather was trying to send you off with his head thug? Would you have just trotted off with him?"

I sighed. "I'm not convinced Jamie has *thugs* in his employ but no, I wouldn't have gone with him. I told you, I don't need a bodyguard." I shook my head. "I'm not up to anymore arguing. If it will make you leave, I promise to catch a ride with Tina."

Dom huffed but nodded. "Fine Ivy, you win for now. I just don't understand why you won't accept what I'm saying. Contrary to what you think, I never lied to you-"

"No, you just neglected to tell me everything. Useful editing, right?"

"It wasn't like that, Ivy, but either way, I'm just trying to look out for you. Why won't you trust me?"

I bit my lip. The note of sincerity rang clear in his voice and my wayward heart was pushing for me to surrender. I resisted. Too many unanswered questions lay between us and until they were resolved, I'd keep my heart. "Dom, I know you mean well, but please, just give me a little space, okay?"

My shoulders sagged with relief as he nodded and strode to the door. If he'd wavered or protested much longer, I would have caved in and followed my heart and that was the last thing I needed.

I moved through the kitchen, avoiding Tina's curious gaze, and headed straight for the office, acknowledging that determination, reason, and dumb luck were likely the only way I'd navigate the minefield I was standing in.

A Close Call

Ivy

I slammed the walk-in cooler door shut and stomped back to the stove, studiously avoiding Tina's eyes. I'd managed to dodge my friend's questions for over a week and with luck, I'd avoid them for a few more.

The Cosmic Café was off to a great start. Since opening, we'd had capacity crowds all day, every day. I only hoped it would continue after the influx of St. Patrick's Day tourists left town.

With the need to keep soup kettles full, muffins baked, and salads prepped, I'd been able to keep myself from dwelling too hard on Jamie's behavior on opening night but the continued fight with myself over investigating Dom's allegations was tearing me apart and making me absent-minded.

And then there was Dom. His arrival at the Cosmic had sparked my anger but also my desire. Anger managed to remain strong while he stood before me, but the desire was now taking the lead. During the day, I stayed busy, and as long as I avoided long conversations with the curious Tina, Dom stayed out of my thoughts.

However, the long nights were another story. I lay in bed, staring at the blinking red light on the alarm keypad thinking about Dom, the ring, and Jamie. While my mind dwelled on the wild story Dom had told, my treacherous body replayed every kiss and caress. I could ignore the desire he ignited if only my heart wasn't involved.

I mocked myself for my foolish longings. Every time I closed my eyes, his face rose before me and I remembered his concern for my comfort, his gallantry, his smile, and the way his dark eyes twinkled when he teased me.

But then his perfidy would rear its ugly head and I found it hard to believe I'd ever entertained the notion that he was a keeper. In light of the words that came from his mouth, it seemed my track record for attracting duds was far from over.

His every action during our date now seemed suspect but try as I might, I couldn't get him out of my head. Of course, he wasn't making it easy. I'd asked for space; I should have been more specific.

He called at least twice a day, though I refused the calls at the café and let the answering machine pick up at home. He was also sending flowers. He seemed to have an uncanny knack for timing deliveries for when I was least busy.

Every afternoon another arrangement or potted plant arrived with a note that begged forgiveness and another chance, not that I read them, but I hadn't been able to keep Tina from doing so.

I shook my head and tried to concentrate on the pot of potato soup I was supposed to be creating; the last thing I needed was another mishap.

Oil and butter were combined in a sauté pan and set to heat while I diced the leeks, celery, and carrots. Once the fats rippled, I added the vegetables, gave the pan a shake, and then lowered the heat. I walked to the sink and frowned.

"Tina?"

Tina came around the corner carrying a tray of fresh-ly baked oatmeal raisin muffins. "Yeah Ivy, Whatcha need?"

My hands went to my hips. I swallowed my irritation and then looked at Tina. "Where are my peeled potatoes?"

Tina cocked an eyebrow. "Did you ask the prep cook for peeled potatoes?"

I huffed. "How else would I make ..." I stopped, realizing my mistake. My shoulders sagged. "I didn't leave Pete a note, did I."

Tina shook her head. "Not that I'm aware of." She set the tray of muffins on the counter and hugged me. "Look, Ivy, it's clear your brain is otherwise occupied. No, don't tell me to mind my business cuz you know I can't."

She grinned. "This is the third time this week you've messed up. Have you forgotten the minestrone missing pasta and the flat, rubbery ham and cheese muffins?" Tina walked across the kitchen and turned off the burner. "Just listen, okay?"

I sighed and nodded, knowing my friend was right.

"Okay, so whatever happened with that gorgeous security guy is eating at you. Why don't you go sort it out before you create a disaster I can't fix?"

My mouth dropped open at Tina's blunt words but then I shook my head and flashed a weary smile. "Just what culinary nightmare could I create that the great Chef Tina couldn't repair?"

Tina smirked. "Better not to find out, don't you think?" She waved me from the room. "Just go on and take care of whatever is eatin' at you so we can get back to runnin' the Cosmic. I'll get Pete on the spuds and finish the soup."

I removed my chef's coat and tossed it into the linen bag. "You win, but I'm not leaving. I'll be in the office finishing up next week's order if you need me."

A sarcastic snort followed me from the room. I sank onto my office chair and powered up the computer. Tina was right. My attention was not on the Cosmic Café.

Dom and his suspicions. I didn't need any of that crap weighing me down right now but there it lay. I was at a loss as to how to rid myself of it.

I clicked on several bills to pay and followed the prompts until the account was settled. I sighed. The only way to ease my mind was to put Dom's theories to rest, yet I shied from taking the first step.

To investigate at all seemed to give his accusations credence. It also seemed disloyal to the man who'd become like a father to me. I was painfully aware of all that Jamie had done for me.

Without his investment, I wouldn't have the Cosmic, not to mention the spacious house he rented to me for next to nothing. I couldn't go digging into his life and possibly derail his political ambitions just to satisfy an

RING OF LIES

obsessed ex-cop, no matter how much he haunted my dreams.

Still, too many questions lay unanswered, and my mind wouldn't let it rest. Coincidences were piling up, and if I factored in my godfather's remarks about the ring and the look I'd seen on his face, it was impossible to push the suspicions aside.

I bit my lip and closed down the computer. If I wanted any peace, I'd have to lay my concerns to rest, once and for all. I sighed and went back to the kitchen.

I leaned against the wall and watched my small staff bustle around the immaculate kitchen. Tina hadn't lied, I had made some dumb mistakes lately. Mistakes a fledgling restaurant could ill afford.

There was no avoiding it. To clear my mind, I'd have to find the truth about the past, no matter the personal cost. I pushed away from the wall and cleared my throat.

Tina turned from the stove. "Hey Ivy, feeling better?"

I nodded. "Yeah, but I'm kind of tired. Do you mind if I leave a bit early?"

Tina stirred a large can of evaporated milk into the pot of simmering potatoes and leeks. "Sure Ivy, we're on the back side of the lunch crowd and I'm scheduled to work the supper shift. Go on, take a break. St. Paddy's Day will be a busy one, better rest while you can."

I laughed. "Yeah, last days to breathe before P-Day. Oh, did I remember to tell you, that I added Reuben

141

Casserole to the menu? Not Irish, per se, but it has corned beef."

Tina grinned. "Yeah, you told me. I ordered rye flour to make the bread and I'm slow cooking sauerkraut, so everything is ready."

She waved a hand at me. "Now scoot. Enjoy the rest of the day!"

I gave her a half-hearted smile and grabbed my coat. I walked aimlessly through the park, unsure of where to start. Finally, I sat on a bench in front of the fountain and stared at the fanciful statues spouting water turned green for the St. Patrick's Day festivities, while I considered the little I knew.

I glanced down at my finger. Everything seemed to hinge on the ring. Dom swore it was real, some kind of antique, so perhaps a jeweler was the place to start. I sighed and started walking again. I wandered down an azalea-lined path, absently admiring the brilliant hues while I turned over all the questions and coincidences.

If Aunt Fey's boyfriend had murdered Dom's mother, then it was possible he also stole the ring. That could explain how Fey had ended up with it. But why would she hide it? Did she know?

I shook my head. Whatever else my aunt had been, she wasn't likely to conceal something like a robbery or a murder. I sighed. Perhaps I hadn't known Aunt Fey as well as I'd thought. According to Dom, I certainly was wrong about Jamie.

The murder of my aunt weighed heavy on my mind. Dom's assertion that the break-in at my house and the attempted mugging were linked to the ring made me wonder. Had the person who wanted the ring discovered that Aunt Fey had it? Was that why she was killed? It seemed likely, but how would the murderer have known about it? The ring had been hidden in the bank vault.

My eyes widened as a thought occurred. The ring wasn't the only thing Aunt Fey hid at the bank. I mentally reviewed all that I'd found in the box.

Aside from the ring, there'd been a bunch of old receipts and legal documents, but what they could have to do with any of the things I suspected was beyond me.

The only other questionable items were the newspaper clippings. I vaguely recalled one of the headlines referring to a robbery.

With what I now knew, the clipping made sense. But everything had taken place twenty years ago. I wondered where to start my search for answers.

A car horn sounded on the road nearest the path, diverting my attention. I looked up and my gaze came to rest on the three-story brick townhome that housed the Savannah Historic Society.

I smiled. I turned and started jogging home. A glance at my watch showed it to be almost two. Plenty of time to grab the clippings and start the search.

Ivy

"Come on, Sergeant!" I gritted my teeth and gave a gentle tug on the cat's leash. The bratty cat ignored me and continued to hiss at the man jogging in place on the street corner.

I sighed and walked back down the brick steps to scoop him up. I tightened my grip on the wriggling mass of fur and trotted back up to the historical society's door. Fervently hoping they wouldn't mind the cat, I stepped inside.

A rush of warm air carried the scent of dust and old leather to my nose. I tucked the cat into his basket before peeking around a stained-glass pocket door. I looked around, noting the dark woodwork and period furniture.

The place was decked out like a late Victorian parlor, filled with horsehair sofas, rows of glass-fronted bookcases, and tables filled with old picture frames and object d'art. The only thing conspicuously missing were warm bodies.

I adjusted the basket in my arms then turned back toward the foyer, only to jump as I came face to face with a wizened old man. I gasped and Sergeant stuck his head out of his basket and growled.

"Oh! Goodness, you startled me."

"I'm sorry, dear. It's so quiet in here I suppose I try to match it." The old man smiled and offered his hand. "I'm Ambrose Williams, head archivist. Have you come to do research?"

I accepted his hand. "I'm Ivy Michaels, and yes, I was hoping to find information on some things I found while settling my aunt's affairs. I'm not sure why she kept them."

His old brown eyes lit up. "How nice, I'll help if you like. I love a mystery!"

I smiled. "I'll take all the help I can get but I'm not sure how much of a mystery you'll experience. They're just some old newspaper clippings."

He chuckled and directed me to follow him down the wide hallway. "Ah, a jumping-off point then. Sometimes the most innocuous things can lead to fascinating dis-coveries."

He stepped into a small room just off the stairwell. "Please, have a seat and make yourself comfortable. Can I get you something? Tea? Or perhaps a saucer of cream for the kitty?"

I bit my lip. I'd thought he hadn't noticed the cat. "Um ... I meant to ask if it was all right to bring Sergeant in. I tried to leave him at home, but he was persuasive.

I've been working a lot and he's lonely. When he feels ignored, he can get ... destructive."

Mr. Williams waved a hand. "Don't trouble yourself. I've two Himalayan Persians at home. Beautiful creatures but the devil of a temper!"

He tottered toward an alcove and disappeared behind a thick red curtain, appearing moments later with a wooden tea tray. "There we are. A bit early for tea but it isn't often I get to take it with a pretty young woman, so we'll make an exception, hmm?"

I smiled and accepted the delicate white China cup and saucer. A meow of protest sounded from the floor. I nudged the basket with my foot and whispered, "Hush, Sergeant."

The old man grinned and poured a small puddle of cream into a shallow bowl. "I believe he heard me mention this." He set the saucer beneath the desk. "Let him out, dear. I assure you it's fine, and we'll have no peace if you don't."

I laughed and flipped the latch on the basket. The ball of fur was out in a flash. He ran straight for the cream, sniffed once, and then started to lap.'

Mr. Williams smiled. "There, now L'Enfant terrible is content and we can begin our quest."

I grinned and pulled the yellowed papers from my bag. I leaned across the wide mahogany desk and extended my hand. Ambrose gasped and his hand shook, slopping tea over the side of his cup.

"Mr. Williams, are you all right?"

He set his cup down and nodded. "I'm fine, dear, just startled." His warm brown eyes were alive with curiosity as he motioned toward my hand. "I wonder if I might see that ring you're wearing?"

I swallowed hard. I'd come for answers, though I hadn't expected them regarding the ring. Still, it seemed to draw a lot of attention. Some of it was unwanted and dangerous, and knowing the truth about it could only make me safer.

I slowly twisted the thin gold band, working it off of my finger. "Are you knowledgeable about jewelry, Mr. Williams?"

The old man turned the ring to the light and stared at it, frowning fiercely. After several minutes, he blinked and met my gaze. "I'm sorry, dear, did you ask me something? I'm afraid I was lost in thought."

Bemused, I shook my head and watched as the old man's eyes closed. He sat perfectly still except for small movements of his lips. I leaned forward, trying to hear what he mumbled but no sound reached my ears. Concerned, I started to speak when his eyes popped open, and he grinned. "I have it!"

I gave him a nervous smile and then watched as he set the ring onto his desk blotter, before walking over to a row of shelves. "Ah ..., here it is."

He extracted a large, leather-bound book and then took the seat beside me. "Hand me the ring, dear, won't you?"

I moved to comply as he flipped through the pages of the book. He took the ring from me, examined it closely, then handed it back and set the open book before me. He tapped the page on the right. "There it is. The minute I saw it, I knew."

I cocked my head to the side and peered at the page laid out in neat columns reminiscent of a newspaper. In the corner was a small,thumbnail-sized picture bearing a striking resemblance to the ring in my hand.

I bit my lip, scanned the short article, and then stared at the old man. "I ... you think my ring used to belong to Mary Gibbons?"

His old face was awash with excitement. "I do indeed. If you'll turn it just so ...there, you see?"

I squinted and could just make out the tiny letters engraved along the inside of the ring's band. "*Dum Spiro* ... what?"

He grinned. "*Dum Spiro, Spero*. It's Latin for 'While I breathe, I hope.' It was the Gibbons family motto. I did a lot of research on them when I was asked to assist in the ring's authentication."

"When was this?"

"Hmmm?" Mr. Williams stared at the ring then jerked his gaze away to meet mine. "When? Oh, well, I believe we started work in 1998? Yes, I believe that is when the items were found; of course, I could be wrong- "

"What was found, Mr. Williams? I'm afraid I don't understand. I feel like I've walked in on the third act of a play."

"Oh, my dear, I am sorry! I forget it is all so much history to you young people." He scratched his head and took a sip of tea. "Now then, I'll start at the beginning, shall I?"

I smiled and nodded. Finally, I would have some answers.

Mr. Williams sat back in his chair and patted his thigh. To my amazement, Sergeant jumped onto his lap, circled twice, then settled and began to purr. *Would wonders never cease?*

"Now then, it was just about this time in 1998 that renovation work at the Gibbons House uncovered a secret compartment buried within a wall. A cache of family items was recovered. It was all very exciting, I assure you."

I grinned at his enthusiasm. "What all was found and why was it hidden in the first place?"

"Well, as best I can recall, there was a silver tea service, a christening gown, some other family treasures, and of course, the blue diamond." He scratched Sergeant's chubby cheeks and then continued. "I was working for the Telman Museum at the time and my job was to examine and authenticate the tea service so that is what I remember best. Anyway, after much research, I discovered the reason behind the hidden compartment. It was because of the War you know."

I chuckled. In the South, he could only mean the Civil War, or as all good Southerners called it, The War of Northern Aggression. "The family hid the items from the Yankees?"

Mr. Williams nodded. "Yes, but not just any Yankees, Sherman's Yankees. When the devil occupied Savannah, he and his officers claimed many of our finest houses for their personal use and Union headquarters. Sherman himself stayed at the Green-Meldrim house and the Pink House was used by General York."

He winked. "The Gibbons House fell to a group of lower-ranking officers and the Gibbons ladies must have hidden their most prized possessions for fear the louts would steal them." His eyebrows rose to meet his hairline. "They did that, you know. So many of the South's finest treasures ended up gracing the homes of the northern aggressors. Why enlisted men even robbed the corpses in Colonial Park Cemetery!"

I suppressed a smile. "Yes, I know. They were horrid to us."

The old man gave a sharp nod. "Quite so! The ladies showed much presence of mind in stashing the items, but unfortunately, they both succumbed to yellow fever without divulging the whereabouts of the treasures. For many years, it was assumed the Union officers had absconded with the goods. It was quite a historical find when we discovered the truth."

"I'm sure it was and how exciting for you to be a part of it."

Mr. Williams smiled. "Oh yes, I was over the moon to be included. Why it was Mr. Brogan himself that requested my services. He'd consulted me on period details when he began the restoration you know."

I sat very still. My stomach rolled as another puzzle piece clicked into place. "James Brogan, the man who's running for congress?"

"Why yes, that's him. He was very involved with the historic district revitalization project you know. Thanks to him, several of our most beautiful landmarks were saved from the wrecking ball."

I nodded and tried to remain calm. "So, Mr. Brogan owned the items found in the house?"

"Technically yes, but he is such a great philanthropist that he gave them to the museum on permanent loan. They're included in an exhibit of Savannah's founding families. Everything but the ring that is."

I forced my features into what I hoped was an unconcerned look. "So, what happened to the ring?"

The look in his eyes turned shrewd. "Well, you should ask, my dear. Tell me, how did you come by it?"

I licked my lips and debated how much to tell him. "Well, my aunt died a couple of weeks ago and it fell to me to sort through her things. The ring was among a box of old papers and those newspaper clippings." I slipped the ring back onto my finger. "I thought it was just costume jewelry."

His eyebrows rose. "I assure you it isn't fake. But you should take it to a jeweler and verify what I've told you." He searched my face for several seconds and then nodded. "The thing is, Ms. Michaels, that ring was stolen just days before it was to become part of the museum's exhibit which makes me wonder how your aunt came by it."

I bit my lip. "Yes, it makes me wonder, too. I think I will follow your suggestion and take it to a jeweler. If it's the real Gibbons diamond, then it belongs to the museum."

He nodded and began to study the clippings I'd brought. "Umm, yes. I would think the Telman Museum would be happy to have the ring, but technically, it would now belong to the insurance company. At least, I would assume so."

I frowned. "Why an insurance company? I thought the items had been given to the museum."

He looked up and shook his head. "Not given on permanent loan. There is a difference. The ownership of all the items still resides with James Brogan and I'm sure he carries insurance on them. The payoff for the ring was big news around here. The Gibbon's ring is almost two full carats and is considered a flawless blue diamond. If my memory serves, its value was close to five hundred thousand dollars. You can imagine what a stir that caused."

My mouth dropped open. I sank back in my chair and stared at him. "I ... are you telling me I've been wearing almost half a million dollars' worth of jewelry?"

Mr. Williams nodded. "If that is the Gibbons diamond you have. Though I'd hazard a guess that it's worth much more today."

I blinked. "Much more ..." I ran a shaking hand through my hair. "That is unbelievable." I snapped the leash onto Sergeant's collar and started to rise. "I think I should be going, Mr. Williams. If I hurry, perhaps I can make it to Park Jewelers before they close. If this ring is real ... well, I certainly don't want to be wearing it."

"Of course, dear, perfectly understandable but wait just a moment." He pushed the newspaper clippings across the desk. "I haven't told you about these."

I sat on the edge of my seat. "Oh yes, I'd forgotten. Can you tell me why these clippings were significant enough to include in a safety deposit box?"

His eyebrows rose. "A safety deposit box? And was the ring also in the box?"

I nodded.

"Hmmm, interesting." He shook his head and smiled. "I'm afraid I can only guess at the significance to your aunt, but I can tell you about the events." He glanced down and shook his head. "Frank Nolan. Hmmm, I'm not familiar with this one. Poor soul murdered in a suspected robbery attempt it seems."

He set the paper aside and turned to the other, pointing one gnarled finger at the two-inch lettering declaring a murder on River Street. "Now this one, that's a different story altogether. This had all of Savannah buzzing."

I nodded. "So violent crime was unusual back then?"

Mr. Williams' lips twitched, and he shook his head. "Alas, I'm afraid not. I would say times were more troubled in Savannah back then than they are today. No, it wasn't the act of murder that had everyone talking, but the victim."

I bit my lip and chose my words carefully. "What, ah, what was so special about her?"

He smirked and pointed to the grainy photo. "*She* was Ms. Lorena Whitaker Riordan. Miss Lorena was from the prominent Whitaker family, and she was quite the socialite until she bucked her daddy and married a shrimper from a little town outside of ... hmmm, Brunswick I believe."

He shook his head. "No matter, Miss Lorena was shunned for her faux pas and dear old daddy cut off her allowance. She had a child, a boy I think, in hopes of regaining her father's favor but it did no good. She divorced her fisherman and tried to enter her social world again, but without her family's money, she could only move on the fringes."

"That's very sad- "

"Oh, you haven't heard the whole tale!" He grinned, obviously relishing his chance to gossip. "Lorena was determined. Since her family name wasn't opening doors, she took another route. Rumors of her affairs were legendary. At one time, she was linked to the mayor and a prominent lawyer. Her most famous affair, however, was also her last. At the time of her death, she was thought to be James Brogan's mistress. She caused quite a scene the night she died."

My heart pounded in my ears and my skin felt clammy. So many things were falling into place, like the links of a chain. I feared what his next words might be, but I forced myself to ask. "What, uh, what kind of scene, Mr. Williams?"

His forehead wrinkled as he considered the question. "As you can imagine, in the days following her murder, everyone was jockeying for the honor of telling the most lurid Lorena tale. Many were passed around, but the winner was the hysterical fit she threw the night she died."

He took a sip of tea. "I can't recall where it took place, but from what I was told, Lorena and James Brogan were seen having a heated discussion. Her voice rose and Mr. Brogan walked away from her. That is when Lorena screamed something about a promise and ran after him. The person who related the story to me said she was crying and clinging to his jacket. Then she started pummeling him. It took several men to pull her off, I understand."

I gulped. Now I had the connection between Dom's mother and James Brogan; and what a connection. Dom would go ballistic when he found out. For a moment, I seriously debated withholding the information, but I knew I couldn't do it. He had a right to know. I would expect the same courtesy if it were my family member. I only wished the bearer of bad news position hadn't fallen to me.

I shook my head and rose from the chair. "Thank you so much, Mr. Williams; you've given me a great deal to think about. My head is spinning." I gathered the clippings and tucked them into my purse before tugging on the leash.

Mr. Williams stood and held the door for me. "I'm glad I could help. Come back and tell me what the police have to say, won't you?"

I turned and frowned at him. "The police?"

A small smile curved his thin lips. "Why yes. Once you verify what I've said about the ring, I'm sure you'll be taking it to the police, right? It is stolen property after all."

My eyes widened. "Good grief, I hadn't thought that far ahead, but yes, I will take it to the police. I might just do that tonight. Lord knows I don't want to be responsible for something this valuable."

I clicked my tongue at the cat. "Come on, boy, let's go."

Mr. Williams walked with me to the front door and glanced at the rapidly darkening sky. He gave me a rueful grin. "I'm afraid a storm is brewing. I'd offer you a ride home, but I take the bus."

I smiled. "Thank you for the offer, but I only live a couple of blocks away. It'll be dark, but I think I can make it before the rain hits."

I set off down the steps, the cat trotting beside me.

"You'd best pick that rascal up or you'll never make it!"

I laughed. "Yes, I know. I'll give him a minute and then shove him back into his basket. He won't like it, but he'll like getting wet even less! Thanks again!" I waved and set off across the street.

A Dicey Situation

Ivy

A brilliant flash of lightning lit the night sky followed by the distant rumble of thunder. I counted the seconds between the two and decided the storm was far enough away to allow a slower pace.

I strolled down the deserted street, watching the cat sniff and explore as I tried to make sense of all that I'd learned. Saying my head was spinning was no exaggeration. Thoughts tumbled through my brain, each one vying for attention and making me feel woozy like I hadn't slept in days.

I tried to focus and piece the events I'd learned from Ambrose Williams together with what I already knew. Frustrated, I rubbed my aching head and decided to leave it alone. Perhaps letting everything simmer on the back burner would bring about a clearer picture.

The huge Live Oak trees above me groaned as a strong gust of wind announced the storm's advancement. I quickened my pace but was stopped short when Sergeant growled and refused to move. I turned to reprimand the cat only to freeze when I saw what was provoking him.

A man stood less than half a block behind me. He was leaning against a Live Oak and a flash of lightning showed him to be a powerfully built man. His body hid all but a few inches of the massive tree's trunk. The hairs on my neck rose and a knot formed in my stomach. There was no sign of a pet, so what was he doing just standing by the curb?

I picked up Sergeant and started walking, fighting the urge to run for about a minute until the alarm bells in my head started to screech.

I broke into a run, clutching the protesting cat against my chest and praying he wouldn't bite me. From behind came the sound of pounding feet, proving my instincts had been sound.

Fat drops of rain began to fall as the wind increased. Jagged bolts of lightning ripped across the black sky while booming thunder shook my already pounding heart. I risked a glance over my shoulder and whimpered. The man was gaining on me.

I struggled to increase my pace. Another block and I'd be at the townhouse. Please God let my neighbors be home. The man's heavy breaths were loud in my ears, and I knew he was close to catching me. My lungs were on fire and my legs were like rubber. Terror propelled me onward.

I was nearing the last cross street when a beefy hand landed on my shoulder, spinning me around and knocking me off balance. My breath whooshed out as I slammed against a parked car.

Sergeant hissed and twisted to be free from my arms as huge hands reached for me. I screamed and closed my eyes. They popped back open as the man in front of me let out a terrified shriek.

I stared, transfixed, as Sergeant growled and tore at the man's face with his claws. The man cursed and struggled to remove the furious cat from his chest.

He raised his arm and I saw the blade of a knife moving toward Sergeant. I screamed, and without thought stepped forward, kicking the man in the crotch.

A high-pitched squeal rent the night as the man sank to his knees. Seizing my opportunity, I pulled Sergeant away and took off.

Minutes later, I was safely inside. I sagged against the door and drew breath after ragged breath, trying to calm my pounding heart and summon the energy to set the alarm. A door slammed in the foyer, and I launched myself toward the keypad.

The blinking red light gave me a measure of security, but I was far from calm. Dom's concerns about the solarium ran through my mind. I raced into the kitchen, jerked the garden-level door shut, and slid the bolt home.

The action made me feel a little better. I reached for the phone. Hands trembling, I pushed nine and one, then stopped. A break-in, an attempted mugging, and now a man had chased me down the street and assaulted me. I gulped as the incidents coalesced into one thought.

Dom was right. Someone was after me and it was more than likely because of the ring on my finger. I hung up and leaned against the counter. If I called the police, would I have to reveal my suspicions? It would be the prudent thing to do, but what did I know really? It was simply speculation on my part.

An image of the smirking and suspicious young Detective Adkins rose in my mind. I didn't relish the idea of involving the police and confessing what I'd found in my aunt's belongings, at least not until I had proof that Aunt Fey had committed no crimes.

I ran a hand through my hair and looked around the kitchen as thoughts whirled in my overwrought mind. Dark red streaks on the white marble tiles drew my attention.

My eyes widened when I saw Sergeant's fat paw print outlined in rusty red. I gasped and called for the cat. A loud meow signaled his presence on the other side of the center island. I walked around the cabinets, dropping to my knees beside him.

Ignoring his head butts and demands for food, I ran my hands along his body, checking for injuries. Finding nothing amiss, I wet a paper towel and wiped the blood from his paws.

I scratched his chubby cheeks, then pulled the plastic tub of dry cat food from the cabinet. Pushing Sergeant aside, I reached for the scoop. The sound of metal scraping metal drew my attention. I filled the cat's bowl and then stared at the glittering ring on my finger.

My hand shook as realization sunk in. The facts were piling up and I couldn't deny them any longer. The big blue stone on my hand was a blue diamond worth a ton of money and someone was going to extraordinary lengths to get it from me.

Dom insisted that someone was my godfather, but my heart refused to let me go that far. All I could accept was that someone was after me and the odds were good it was because of the ring. Which meant, I wasn't going to be caught dead in the thing-literally or figuratively.

I twisted the band from my finger and then looked around for a hiding place. My gaze lit on the open cat food bin. I grinned and grabbed a plastic storage bag from the drawer. No way anyone would think to look for a blue diamond under a mound of kibble.

A gust of wind rattled the windows and the lights flickered. My mouth went dry at the thought of riding the storm out alone and in the dark. I closed the plastic tub and went to gather alternative lighting.

Minutes later, I looked over the dozen-odd candles assembled like soldiers across the table and sighed. Hopefully, there would be no need for them, but it paid to be prepared.

I poured myself a glass of wine and tried to settle my frazzled nerves but the howling wind and frequent thunder made that impossible. So much for a restive day off. I mentally replayed everything the old man at the historical society had told me.

Unfortunately, everything seemed to be leading to Aunt Fey. My mind rebelled at the thought. My aunt had been flighty and a bit rash, but I knew beyond a doubt she'd been no thief. Which left me with Dom's theory but that seemed even harder to accept. Jamie loved me;

surely, he wouldn't send someone to harm me. But if not him, who?

Bile rose in my throat as I relived my flight from the man on the street. Again, I thought of calling the police, but what could I say besides a big man had chased me down Gwinnet Street, and when he caught me, the cat scared him off. At best, they'd dismiss the incident as an encounter with a mentally ill homeless person and tell me to call if anything else occurred.

I could tell them about the ring, the past crimes, and the series of violent incidents plaguing me but again, I had nothing but speculation. I refilled my glass and wandered to the bank of windows overlooking the courtyard garden, leaning my head against the cool glass.

The rain was coming down in buckets now and thunder rattled the windowpanes. The lush foliage was cloaked in utter darkness illuminated by flashes of lightning that cast huge and grotesque shadows along the brick wall and pathways. I shivered and thought again of my close call. Thank God for Sergeant, the attack cat.

I took a sip of wine and half turned when movement by the wrought iron garden gate caught my eye. I leaned closer to the window and strained to see through the driving rain. I shook my head, convinced it must have been a trick of the light. I sighed and wandered to the fridge, hoping to find something edible.

I grabbed a couple of eggs, and some cheese then froze as lightning flashed, thunder shook the room, and the lights went out.

"Oh, crud! So much for dinner." I set the food down by the sink and then felt my way along the counter, frantically searching for the box of matches. I sighed as my hand closed over the box. Now to make it to the table without tripping over anything.

I took two cautious steps in the direction of the breakfast nook then screamed as Sergeant let out an angry hiss. "Oh! Sorry, baby, did I get your tail?"

A low growl answered the question. I slid my feet across the tiles until I collided with the metal leg of a chair. With a sigh, I patted the tabletop until I encountered a candle. Blue flame erupted as I scratched the match along the edge of the box. A soft glow lit the room and guided my path to the bedroom.

Snuggled under a blanket with the cat beside me, I wondered how long the lights would be out. From the sounds of the storm, I guessed it'd be all night.

Normally, I'd use the time to catch up on sleep, but the events of the day had me keyed up. Every noise outside made me jump and think of the crazed man who'd chased me.

I lay in the dark, stroking the cat and trying to calm my raw nerves and active imagination. I stared at the warm red glow of the alarm system and remembered what Dom had said. Help was a yell away; all I had to do was push the blue button. That knowledge, combined with the steady rumble of Sergeant's purrs lulled me. My eyelids fluttered and in minutes I was fast asleep.

Ivy

I bolted upright in bed and tried, without success, to convince myself that what I'd heard was not the sound of breaking glass. I closed my eyes and listened closely.

My heart pounded in my ears, but I could still detect the unmistakable sound of footsteps in the room downstairs. Mouth dry and hands shaking, I reached out to the security keypad, but before I could mash the button, a high-pitched wail filled the house.

I grabbed my cell phone and leaped from the bed, heading for the garden doors. I turned the lock and stepped out onto the balcony in time to see a large, shadowy figure scurrying through the garden gate. The phone rang.

"Hello?"

"Ms. Michaels. This is Savannah Security Systems. We show your alarm has been activated. Is everything all right?"

Shaking and dripping wet, I huddled under the eaves and tried to talk around the lump in my throat. "No! Someone tried to break in!"

"Hold on, ma'am. We're sending the police."

There was a pause then another, familiar voice, came on the line. "Ivy! Ivy, what's going on?"

I sagged against the glass door. "Dom! Oh God, Dom. There was this man ... he chased me home. Sergeant attacked him ... I woke up, breaking glass-"

"Ivy! Ivy, calm down. Look, the police are on the way and I'm right behind them. Where are you now?"

I drew a ragged breath. "I'm out on the balcony. I ..., I was afraid ... the alarm went off- "

"Look, sweetheart. Just stay where you are, someone might still be in the house- "

I whipped around, staring into my darkened bedroom. "Oh my God ..."

"Calm down. Whoever it was probably left at the sound of the alarm, but it's better to be safe. I'm leaving now. I'll be there in ten minutes."

I bit my lip to stop the trembling and sank onto my knees. "Okay, just ... please hurry!"

Kiss and Make Up

Dom

I spent the short drive to Ivy's house cursing myself for a fool. If anything happened to her, it'd be my fault. I'd known she was in danger and that Brogan wouldn't stop until he had the ring. Yet I'd allowed Ivy's injured feelings to sway my judgment. She'd asked for time, and like a fool, I'd given it to her. Now she'd almost paid the ultimate price.

Flashing blue and red lights lit up the night as I turned onto her street. I whipped into a parking spot and jogged down to Ivy's townhome. Seeing a group of cops in the garden, I slipped through the gate. A uniformed officer halted me before I'd taken three steps. "Sir, this is a crime scene- "

"It's all right, officer; I'm with the alarm company."

The cop squinted in the darkness for several seconds and then thrust out his hand. "Dom Riordan, right?"

I frowned and tried to see the man's face in the low light. "Yeah, I'm Dom-hey! Bobby Arnold, how ya been?"

The officer chuckled. "I've been all right. Heard you started a security company after you left the force. You always show up when a customer's alarm is tripped?"

I laughed and shook my head. "No, but this one is my girlfriend's." I peered around the man, catching a glimpse of a crime tech dusting a broken window. "Is she all right?"

Officer Arnold nodded. "Yeah, she's okay. She's upstairs givin' a statement. She's soaking wet and shook up, but the perp was gone when we got here."

I blew out a breath. "I'm glad but I wish you'd caught the bastard."

"I noticed she had another break-in a week ago."

I nodded absently. "Hmmm, nothing was stolen the first time; maybe he was interrupted and decided to try his luck again." I searched the upstairs windows for a glimpse of Ivy, but the house was too dark. "Look, it was great seeing you again, but I'm worried about my girl. You think I can go in?"

"Hmm? Oh, sure but go in the front. Tech guys are still processing down here."

I nodded and headed around to the front. A few minutes later and a short conversation with another buddy and I was standing in the shadow-filled living room.

I looked around, trying to determine where the voices were coming from. "Ivy?"

"Dom!"

At her soft cry, I turned toward the kitchen. A blur of motion and she was pressed against my chest. Hot tears ran down the side of my neck and her body trembled in my arms.

"Hey, easy now. I'm here." I stroked her hair and murmured nonsense until she quieted. I set her away from me and tilted her chin, so our eyes met. "Better now?"

Ivy hiccupped and nodded.

I smiled at her, then wrapped an arm around her waist and guided her back to the kitchen. I groaned inwardly as I caught sight of the female officer scribbling notes at the table amidst a cluster of lit candles. Of all the cops who could have pulled Ivy's call, it had to be Dena Carter.

Ambitious suck-up, she'd taken immense pleasure in assisting IA when James Brogan had filed his complaint. I wondered what she was doing on the street. Last I had heard, she was sitting for the detective exam. I snorted. Brown-nosing could only take idiots so far.

She looked up as we entered. "Ms. Michaels-" She stopped when she caught sight of me. Her lips thinned into a hard line. She fixed me with a cold stare and then turned back to Ivy. "Can we finish the interview now?"

Ivy nodded. "Yes, but I think I've told you everything."

Carter's gaze flicked back to me and then she nodded. "Yes ma'am. I just want to be sure we haven't overlooked anything." She looked down at her notes. "You arrived home around seven and you didn't find anything suspicious. The lights went out, so you went to bed, and then you were awakened by the sound of breaking glass. The alarm went off and you saw someone run out through the garden gate. Is that correct?"

Ivy nodded. "Yes, that's what happened."

The officer's eyes narrowed, and she looked from Ivy to me and then back to Ivy. I stiffened. Suspicion was clear on her face.

She jerked her head toward the kitchen floor. "We found some reddish streaks on the floor over by the door that leads to the garden. The tech says it's blood."

Ivy frowned then her expression cleared. "Oh, with everything that's happened I forgot. Sergeant, that's my cat, he cut his foot on something just before the lights went out. I wiped his paws, but I forgot to do the floor."

The officer studied Ivy's face for several seconds then she shrugged. "I'll let the tech know then." She glared at me and then headed to the door. "I'll file the report and the tech's looking for fingerprints. We'll let you know if we find anything."

Ivy opened the door. "Thank you, officer."

Ivy closed the door. She turned towards me, her lips forming a shaky smile. "I'm so glad you're here."

I crossed the room and took her into my arms. She relaxed, sighing as I rubbed her back. "I'm sorry. I should have protected you." I gave her a little squeeze. "It won't happen again."

Ivy leaned back and met my gaze. "What are you talking about?" This isn't your fault." She stepped out of my arms and sank onto the couch. "If anything, you tried to warn me. It's my fault ... I didn't listen."

I sat beside her and took her hand. "I should have tried harder to persuade you. I knew the danger; I should have insisted–"

"Dom, stop." Ivy shook her head and smiled softly. "Nothing you could have said would have made me see. I had to find out for myself."

I caught my breath. It sounded like she was accepting what I'd told her. That she believed me. I hadn't realized how much it mattered.

Ivy bit her lip. "I've something I need to tell you. A lot to tell you actually, but ..., I need to warn you that some of it isn't... it isn't very flattering towards your mom."

I stiffened. I read the concern in Ivy's eyes and my heart flipped. I stroked her cheek. "Thank you." I cleared my throat. "Thank you for warning me, but I need to know. Whatever you've found has to be better than not knowing. If it eases your mind, I've always known my mother wasn't a saint."

Ivy flashed a tight smile. "I took some old newspaper clippings to the historical society today."

I listened as Ivy related all that she'd learned about my mother and the ring. The more she talked, the more pieces of the puzzle clicked into place. For years, I'd had fragmented dreams-my mother, dressed in beautiful clothes kissing me goodnight and telling me to be good for old Mrs. Richards, or sobbing in front of the mirror while fat black rivulets of make-up streamed down her face.

I shuddered as the picture that haunted my days and nights rose in my mind.

She stood at the front door dressed in a long red gown. One sleeve was torn, and her bare shoulder was exposed. Her long blonde hair was a tangled mess, parts of it tumbling down her back while the rest teetered precariously from sparkling pins.

Streaks of black on her cheeks showed she'd been crying but I saw no tears. Instead, her eyes glittered with a strange, maniacal light and her voice was high and breathy.

I rubbed the sleep from my eyes. "Where ya going, Mama?"

The musky scent of her perfume tickled my nose as she leaned over and brushed the hair from my face. "Go back to bed, Dommy. I'm just running down the street to meet a friend."

"But Mama, you sent Mrs. Richards home."

My mother didn't answer. She was staring at something inside a small brown box. The sound of crumpling paper filled the room as she rummaged in the box and her lips moved silently as if she were reading.

I moved closer for a better look and then gasped. Lying on a dark green cloth was a ring with a gigantic blue stone. I'd never seen anything so blue or so big, especially not on a ring.

Lorena snapped the lid closed and jerked the box away. "What are you doing? I told you to go back to bed."

The anger in her voice made me step back. I swallowed hard and reminded her about the sitter.

She huffed and flipped the hair from her eyes, primping in front of the hall mirror. "Don't be such a baby. Mrs. Richards is just downstairs, and I'll only be gone a minute. Just lock the door and go to sleep. I'll be here when you wake up, I promise."

I shifted from foot to foot and fought back tears. "All ... all right Mama, but ... but what's in that box?"

Lorena looked at me from the mirror. "Hmmm? Oh, that. Don't you worry about it, baby." She turned and knelt in front of me, I smelled the alcohol on her breath. "That is our ticket out of this dump only it's a secret, okay? Don't tell anyone you saw it."

She gave me a fierce hug and kissed my cheek. "There's Mama's little man. Nightie-night." She patted me on the head and slipped out the door.

"Dom? Are you okay?"

I drew a deep breath and squeezed Ivy's hand. I shook the cobwebs of memory away and tried to smile. "Yeah Ivy, I'm just ... I was remembering the last time I saw my mother." I turned away from the sympathy shining in her eyes and fought to control my emotions.

I hung my head and tried to come to terms with the knowledge that my mother, not Brogan, was the thief-a thief and a whore. I sighed as Ivy began rubbing my back in long, slow strokes.

God, she was sweet. If my world had to be turned upside down, I couldn't think of anyone I'd rather have beside me.

I turned and met her eyes, wondering if we'd have had a chance at a relationship under normal circumstances. I sighed and rubbed a hand across my face.

"Dom? What is it? Are you angry with me?"

I snorted and shook my head. "Angry with you? Ivy, I'm sitting here wishing we'd met in any other way than the tragedy that seems to rule my life!" I stood and began to pace. "The night of our-" I snorted again. "I guess you'd call it a date. That night?" I glanced at her to see her wide blue eyes following my track crisscrossing the room.

She nodded and I continued. "That night, I was ..., I felt closer to you than any woman I've ever met. Fool that I am, I thought we might just have a future, you know? But, as usual, the tragedy that was Lorena Riordan comes roaring in to wreck a good thing!" I swallowed past the lump in my throat and sighed. "I just wish we could start over."

Ivy stood as I passed the couch, putting a hand to my chest. "Dom? I, uh, I was thinking the same way, that night." A self-deprecating little smile curved her full lips and she shrugged. "Kinda figured we didn't have much of a chance after I chewed you out and accused you of, well you know ..."

She pulled me back down onto the couch and held my hand. "Thing is, we were both wrong. You should have told me what you suspected about that ring from the first and I, well I shouldn't have been so quick to defend Jamie."

My eyes widened. "Are you saying you believe what I've said about Brogan?"

She blew out a breath and dropped my hand to tuck a strand of hair behind her ear. "Let's just say there are enough coincidences and connections to make me want more answers."

I smiled. "I can work with that. The first thing we need to do is-"

"Dom."

I frowned as she placed a finger over my lips.

"The first thing we need to do is...," A smile lit her face as she leaned in and replaced her fingers with her lips. She deposited a featherlight kiss before moving back. "Hi, I'm Ivy Michaels, nice to meet you!"

I realized what she was doing and laughed. "Nice to meet you, Ms. Michaels. I'm Dom Riordan, and that was not nearly enough of a greeting."

I pulled her closer and traced the fullness of her lower lip with my tongue, seeking entrance. When she complied, I took full advantage, deepening the tender assault for several minutes before sitting back.

I chuckled as Ivy made a mew of disapproval. The disappointment in her eyes was flattering but I was determined to take things slow this time. I grinned. "Not the time, love." She gave me a puzzled look.

"I would like nothing more than to carry you to that big bed of yours but there are more urgent things on the agenda, don't you think?"

Ivy's lips curled into a reluctant smile. "I suppose you're right..." A mischievous twinkle lit her eyes. "Besides, we've just met!"

I laughed and kissed the tip of her nose. "And what a promising *first meeting* it's turning out to be!"

Deciding she was too much temptation, I moved to the armchair. "Now then," I folded my arms across my chest and directed my 'interrogation' stare at her. "How about you tell me the real story."

Ivy blinked. "What do you mean, I-"

I smirked. "Dena Carter is an idiot. You might be able to brush her off with that nonsense about the cat, but I'm no fool." I raised my eyebrows. "How did the blood get on the floor?"

"Oh!" Ivy snorted. "Um, it really was from the cat, but it isn't his blood. He must have gotten it on him when he attacked the guy in the street."

My stomach clenched and I scooted towards the edge of my seat, grabbing her hand. "What guy on the street? I think you're leaving some things out, Ivy."

She frowned. "I told you on the phone, remember? Right after the alarm went off- "

I rolled my eyes. "I thought you were hysterical and babbling." I waved her to silence as she started to protest. "No matter, just tell me everything now."

Ivy nodded and proceeded to tell me about the man following her home from the historical society. I gritted my teeth. She could have been killed! Brogan was upping the stakes if he'd send someone to rob her in the middle of the street. He was getting desperate, which made him dangerous.

"Dom? Is everything all right? You look angry ..."

I met her gaze, noting the concern and confusion in her expression. I drew a deep breath and tamped down on the anger. "I am angry. At myself." I stood and began pacing her small living room. "I should never have left you alone. I knew Brogan would try again and I should have been with you if anything had happened to you- "

"Dom!" Ivy jumped up from the couch and laid her hand on my arm. "None of this is your fault so quit blaming yourself. I'm the one who is at fault, I didn't believe you." She held up her hand as I started to interrupt.

"It doesn't matter now. What matters is what we do about all of this. I've been thinking and I feel we should turn everything over to the police. Let's get out of this mess and make it their problem."

I rolled my eyes. "Ivy, I appreciate that you want all of this to go away but you're not thinking clearly. We don't have any proof. If anything, what you've discovered points to my mother's and your aunt's guilt, not Brogan's."

Ivy bit her lip. "Dom, have you considered that maybe they were guilty? I mean, you said your mom had the ring the night she died, and we know she fought with Brogan. Maybe she stole it from him." She shook her head and shrugged. "As for Aunt Fey ... well, it disturbs me to think this but, she was dating the man they suspected of your mom's murder. Maybe she hid the diamond for the guy."

I swiped my hand across my face and bit back the sharp remark I'd been about to throw at her. Jealous anger burned through me. Even now, with everything that had happened to her, she refused to see Brogan's guilt. What had the guy done to deserve such loyalty?

I forced my anger down and tried to keep my voice even and detached. "Ivy, that is circumstantial evidence. I admit it's damning, but Brogan is involved. I'm betting he is at the heart of it all. We just need to dig a little deeper. There's something we're missing, some connection we haven't made."

Ivy made an impatient gesture and rolled her eyes. "Has it occurred to you that your obsession with Jamie has blinded you to the truth? The facts speak for themselves, Dom, circumstantial or not."

She shook her head and stalked off to the kitchen. I heard the refrigerator open and the clink of glass. I sighed and followed her. If we were going to solve the mystery, we needed to work together. But we needed to be on the same page, and I was at a loss on how to make that happen.

She stood with her back to me, staring out into the dark garden. Without looking, she motioned toward the counter. "I poured you a glass of wine."

I blew out a breath and grabbed the drink. I downed it in one swallow and then walked over to stand behind her. Her posture was rigid, and tension radiated from her in waves.

I slid my arms around her, pulling her back against my chest. "I don't want to fight with you ... you're all I think about." I smiled into her hair as her body relaxed. "I can't get you out of my mind and I've been crazy with worrying about you."

She sighed. "I don't want to fight with you either and thinking about you keeps me up at night."

I squeezed her and smiled. "Ummm, I like the sound of that, if you're up all night with me."

Ivy chuckled and turned. "Just because I'm admitting my attraction for you doesn't mean I'm backing down. I meant what I said. You are obsessed."

I sighed and rested my forehead against hers. "Look Ivy, I agree I've been blinded by hate for Brogan but that's gone now. This is about you."

She frowned. "Me? How is this about me? I'm not the one who's relentlessly pursuing a man- "

"Ssh ..." I leaned back and put a finger to her lips. "I know. I know what you're thinking. Before all this crap started happening to you, I would have said you were right, but not now." I shook my head. "Ivy, I can't shake the feeling that Brogan is behind all of the violence. Who else could it be?"

She looked away and murmured. "I don't know." She straightened and looked at me. "But I also don't know why it would matter so much to Jaime. I mean, he got the money for the ring so what does it matter–"

"Unless he orchestrated the theft."

Ivy blinked. "You think he was in on it from the start? I don't see ..." she huffed. "What proof do you have?"

I ran a hand through my hair and sighed. "I don't, and that's the problem. I do, however, have the initial insurance adjuster's report. The company paid but they felt something was suspicious. The ring was in Brogan's safe, and they found nothing to indicate a robbery. Whoever removed the ring knew the combination."

I shook my head as Ivy started to speak. "And nothing else was taken. The adjuster on the case tried to investigate further but his superiors pulled him off the case."

Ivy nodded. "Which is why you've always thought Jaime was involved?"

"Yep. What happened to the adjuster happened to me. Brogan pulled strings and I was off the force." I snapped my fingers. "Just like that."

A sad smile twisted her lips. "I'm sorry."

I dropped a light kiss onto her lips. "Don't be. I've moved on to bigger and better things. Just think. If I hadn't left the force, I never would have met you."

Ivy smiled. "I can think of better ways to meet."

I laughed. "So can I but I'm not complaining." I tilted my head to the side and frowned. "You know, I've been thinking."

Ivy walked over to the sink and rinsed our wine glasses. "About what?"

I leaned against the bar and watched her straighten the kitchen. "About your initial break-in. What were they looking for in your office? They rifled through your jewelry box and that makes sense for any burglary, even if I didn't think they were looking for that ring."

I paced the small kitchen. "However, I can't shake my suspicions over the ransacked office. No missing electronics." I scowled. "What self-respecting burglar leaves a laptop? I mean, it was sitting on your desk and all they did was rifle through your papers."

Ivy shrugged. "I don't know. I told you it seemed like malicious kids."

I snorted. "That might have washed before, but now that we know about the ring? I don't buy it. Whoever wants the ring, and I still say it is Brogan-" I held up my hand to forestall her argument. "Whoever it is, they were looking for something among those papers."

Ivy nodded. "That seems logical, but I looked through them. Apart from the newspaper clippings I told you about, the papers were just a bunch of legal documents about my parents' ..." she paused and then shook her head.

I came to stand in front of her. "What? You were going to say something."

Ivy bit her lip. "Nah, it's silly ..."

I shook my head. "No, it's instinct. Just say what came to mind."

Ivy shrugged. "Well, the other papers were receipts and stuff like that. I didn't look carefully but most of them looked like rent receipts, and old electric bills- nothing to do with all of this."

I nodded. "And yet something is bugging you."

She laughed. "Yeah, I guess. I mean, Aunt Fey didn't hold on to things, *literally*, she didn't believe in having stuff from the past; said it weighed the spirit down. So why keep something so innocuous?"

I picked up a candle, grabbed her hand, and headed for the office. "Let's take another look. Maybe you missed something."

Ivy chuckled but allowed me to lead her from the kitchen.

No Stone Unturned

Ivy

Ivy

Dom set the candle onto the bookcase and crossed to my desk, gathering a mess of papers before sitting cross-legged on the floor. He motioned for me to join him and began sorting through the pile. "Just look through these with me. You never know what we might find."

I sighed, wishing I'd never mentioned the oddities with the old papers. While it didn't make much sense for anyone, especially someone like my aunt, to keep such things, I wasn't convinced it meant anything and I'd had a full day; snuggling in the candlelight sounded much better to my weary body.

Still, I sank to my knees and reached for a thick packet of legal-length papers stapled together. "Well, this is the agreement concerning the sale of my parents' home, so I know it's not what you're looking for."

Dom looked up and nodded. "Okay then, start a pile for things that we know aren't suspect." He thumbed through several sheets and tossed them onto the carpet. "All of those are irrelevant as well."

I huffed and added more to the heap. "I've got some random bill receipts and more legal stuff." I ran a hand through my hair. "Dom, this is getting us nowhere. The only papers linked to the ring, or your mom are those newspaper- "

"Hold on Ivy, I may have found something." He held up a torn, dog-eared page. I took the paper from him.

The ink was faded, and water spots marred a corner, but James Brogan's name stood out. It looked to be a document marking a sale. I squinted and tried to make out the writing. I shrugged and handed it back to Dom.

"What is it?" I scooted across the carpet and peered over his shoulder.

He shook his head and studied the paper. "Not sure, but Brogan's name is on it." He pointed to the line labeled

Payee. "See," He pointed at a faded line of text. "It's some sort of receipt. Says Brogan sold-oh my God! This is the receipt for the sale of the diamond!" He moved closer to the candle and continued to decipher. "Four hundred and seventy-five thousand dollars in exchange for a two-carat, flawless blue diamond. Delivery to M. Jong in Narrden, The Netherlands by special courier."

He lowered the paper and stared at me. "It goes on to state the method of money transfer and some other things." He gulped. "I can't believe this, it's proof!"

I bit my lip, reluctant to take his excitement away. I frowned. "I hate to rain on the parade but, is it really?"

Dom scowled. "Of course it is! Are you going to try and defend him aga-"

"Dom! Don't start that again, please." I rolled my eyes, very tired of the assumption I would make excuses for my godfather. If he was guilty, I wanted him punished but I wasn't going to jump to conclusions or go off half-cocked and make accusations against him that might derail him politically and ruin our relationship; I wanted solid evidence and I didn't see the receipt being a smoking gun.

"All I'm saying is, the ring was his property. He was supposed to put it on permanent loan to the museum, but in the end, he could do whatever he liked. Selling it wasn't illegal ..."

Dom cocked an eyebrow and pointed to the top right corner. "You're right, he could legally sell it all day long, but not after it was reported stolen. Look at the date."

I followed his finger and swallowed hard. "August 10, 1992. The ring was stolen before that?"

Dom grinned. "Yep, stolen in 1989, so how was he selling it three years later?"

I took a deep breath, finding no pleasure in the information that my godfather was probably a criminal. "You're right." I shook my head. "But is it enough to go to the police? The ring isn't in his possession and hasn't been for almost twenty years. I would think a good lawyer could argue several points against that paper, regardless of dates."

Dom sighed and dragged a hand through his hair. "Spoken like a good D. A., you missed your calling." He rose and hauled me to my feet. "Guess I jumped the gun. Still, combined with more evidence, it forms a damning case."

I extinguished the candle, then moved closer and wrapped my arms around him, squeezing gently. "I'm disappointed too, though probably not for the same reasons as you," I smirked. "I wish it were the magic pill that made all of this go away." I yawned. "Where do we go from here?"

Dom rubbed my back and I melted against him. "Keep doing that and I'll keep you."

He chuckled and added pressure at the base of my spine as he nuzzled my neck. "I'm not sure what our next move is, I'll have to sleep on it."

I grinned and pressed closer, meeting his gaze. "Sure sleep is what you had in mind?"

Dom grinned. "Well, I might be persuaded to explore other options." His smile faded. "Ivy, I'm sorry about what happened before. I never meant to hurt you and all along I had doubts that you were tied up in this mess." He sighed. "Can you forgive me?"

I closed my eyes for a moment and then met his gaze. "We've already covered this, remember? But yes, I forgive you. It hurt to think you were using me and that you suspected me of such terrible things. However, I can see now why you would jump to such conclusions." I shrugged. "In your place, I would have done the same, though I wouldn't have made love with you- "

"Ivy, I swear, that was never part of my plan!"

I cocked an eyebrow at him but nodded that I accepted his statement.

He sighed. "From the moment I saw you standing in the kitchen doorway at the Cosmic, I wanted you. I was fantasizing and planning to ask you out but then I saw Brogan." He shook his head. "That threw me. I hate the guy and you were so friendly with him." He shrugged. "Even that didn't turn me off completely, but when you held out your hand and I saw that ring ... man, you have no idea what that did to me."

Thinking back to that day my eyes widened. "I can guess. You looked like you might pass out, but I put it down to illness." I tightened my arms around his waist. "We've agreed to start over. I mean, not over, we can't pretend we haven't ... um, you know ... but ..."

He grinned. "Yeah, I know, and I don't want to pretend that didn't happen." He bent his head and captured my lips. I leaned forward and increased the pressure.

Dom groaned and twined his fingers in my hair. He broke from my lips to press moist kisses across my cheeks and down my neck. I tilted my head and allowed him greater access, wondering if I should let the moment run its course or call a halt.

On the one hand, we were starting over and should probably take it slow, but on the other ... my stomach fluttered as he ran his hands down my back.

Making up my mind, I pulled back slightly and cleared my throat.

Dom opened his eyes and met my gaze. "What's wrong?"

I shook my head and smirked. "Not a thing but ..." I grabbed his hand and backed toward the door. "My bed is more comfortable."

Ivy

I stretched and opened my eyes to find Dom standing beside the bed toweling his hair dry. I smiled and reached for him.

Dom laughed and stepped back. "Ah ah, none of that. We've got work to do."

I pouted and sat up against the headboard. "What kind of work?"

Dom grinned and swatted my legs with the towel. "It's Saint Patrick's Day, in case you've forgotten, and I'm assuming your café will do a brisk business. There is also the matter of Brogan to deal with."

I ran a hand through my hair and swung my legs from the bed. "Crap! I gotta get to the Cosmic. Tina will be swamped with work."

I grabbed some clothes and headed to the bathroom. Turning on the shower, I adjusted the temperature and then hollered through the open door. "What are you going to do today?"

I stepped under the stream of water and soaped my hair and then jumped as Dom pulled the curtain back. "Dom! You're going to get water everywhere!"

He laughed "A little water never hurt anyone."

I laughed and shooed him away. He made a face but pulled the curtain closed. "Look Ivy, I'm going to drop you at the café and then check-in at my office."

I rinsed my hair and shut off the water, pulling back the curtain. "Okay, maybe we can meet up later? Hand me a towel, please."

I took the towel from him and dried off, thinking I could get used to having him around; it was ... cozy.

"So, you'll be working at your office all day?"

Dom shook his head. "Not much to do today, Savannah is too much of a madhouse on Saint Pat's to get any work done. Just gonna check on a few projects and then I'm going to do a little investigating on our mystery attacker."

I moved into the bedroom and sat at the dressing table. I looked at Dom. "Why can't I help you with that?"

He finished buttoning his shirt and then grinned. "Because."

I stuck my tongue out at him and pulled a comb through my hair. "What kind of answer is that?"

He grinned. "The only one you're going to get." He crossed to the door and winked at me. "Hurry up and get dressed, I'm going to make coffee."

I twisted my hair into a knot and searched for clothes, raising my voice so Dom would hear. "I hate to tell you, but the only thing here is herbal tea."

I laughed as his groan drifted down the hall.

A few minutes later, I found Dom in the kitchen petting Sergeant and munching dry cereal. I shook my head and poured a glass of pomegranate juice. "I have milk, you know."

He snorted. "You call that stuff milk?"

I laughed. "Yes, it's made from almonds and it's good for you."

He rolled his eyes. "So is cow's milk." He finished off the cereal and patted the cat's head. "Good little watch cat. I forgot to thank you for rescuing your mistress yesterday."

I grinned. "He is a good boy, but any minute now he's gonna bite you. He's just being friendly because he wants to be fed."

Dom jerked his hand away. "Little beast."

He moved away so I could fill Sergeant's bowl and then laughed when I pulled the plastic bag out of the bin. "You hid the ring under the cat food?"

I smirked. "Don't laugh. Can you think of a better place? No way Sergeant would let a stranger paw through his food."

Dom laughed. "Point taken." He pulled his car keys from his pocket. "You about ready? I can hear the bands tuning up. If we don't get going now, they'll close the roads off."

I patted Sergeant's head and nodded. "Yep, let's go."

The sound of music and laughter floated in the wind as we made our way to Dom's car. I mentally ran through my day, deciding what I wanted to accomplish and listing priorities.

My planning led in a circular fashion back to how Dom had said his day was going to run. I buckled in and then crossed my arms, staring at him.

Dom turned the key and then glanced at me. "What?"

"I'm just wondering why I can't go with you. I think we should work on this together."

Dom rolled his eyes and then turned his attention to guiding the car into traffic. "Ivy you admitted that you'll be busy today, and honestly? I don't want you involved any more than you are."

He checked oncoming traffic and then maneuvered a turn before continuing. "Things are getting hotter, and it isn't safe."

I huffed. "I can take care of myself. Besides, I'm the one who found the connection between Jamie and your mom. I should be allowed to see this through."

Dom shook his head. "You've done your part; now let me do mine. All I'm going to do today is make some calls and see if I can get a buddy on the force to do me a favor or two."

"Like what?"

He glanced at me and then concentrated on the road. "Um ... what I have in mind is barely legal, so I'd rather not tell you."

My mouth dropped open. "There's no way you're going to drop something like that and then not tell me."

Dom sighed. "I've been thinking about everything we discussed last night. We don't have any direct proof that Brogan was involved. We need him to confess or at least slip up enough to point me in the right direction."

I snorted. "You think you're going to waltz right up to James Brogan and get a confession? I'd like to see that."

He shook his head. "No smart ass, I don't see that happening. What I do see is an informant rooting around, getting close to his operation and passing along some intel."

I bit my lip and stared at the throngs of people jostling for positions along the parade route. Business should be brisk, and I'd be over the moon if it weren't for the ring business; it hung over my head like a dark cloud, and Dom's plan wasn't going to bring blue skies any time soon. "That could take months."

Dom pulled up in front of the café and looked at me. "You got a better idea?"

I shook my head and turned in the seat, ready to tell him to just leave it all alone for the day and we'd talk about it later but a knock on my window derailed whatever I was going to say.

I looked over my shoulder to see a cop motioning the car to move. "Can't stop here folks, get a move on."

I sighed and stepped from the car, leaning in the open door. "Look, I can't concentrate right now. Let's just think on it a little, okay?"

The cop glared at me and the car behind us laid on his horn. I scowled and slammed the car door. I tapped on the window and waited until Dom rolled it down. "Just wait until this crazy day is over. We'll talk it all through- "

"Go to work, Ivy, and leave all of this to me." Another blast from a car horn cut him off.

He grinned and blew me a kiss. "Gotta run, babe. I love you, have a great day!"

My mouth dropped open as he inched back into traffic. I shook my head, all thoughts of the mystery gone, replaced by three little words. I stepped off the curb and yelled into the open window.

"Dom wait! Did you just say- "

Dom laughed, gave a jaunty wave, and drove off. I sighed and watched him fade into the sea of cars and people. I walked toward the café grumbling. Stubborn man, but then weren't they all? He might be a stubborn jackass, but apparently, he was my stubborn jackass.

I walked inside, mulling over his parting words. I'd clearly heard him say he loved me. Despite the casual delivery of the words, I didn't feel like Dom was the type to throw them around lightly. But how did I feel about him?

Lost in thought, I walked into the kitchen and came face to face with Tina. I stifled a groan. The oh-so-perceptive Tina was the last person I needed at the moment.

Tina gave me a long look and then cocked one eyebrow. "What's wrong."

My shoulders drooped. True to form, Tina had read me like a book. I decided to brazen it out and hope my lying skills were equal to the task of bluffing my best friend. I straightened my shoulders and tried to clear my face of all expression. "Nothing's wrong. How are lunch preparations going?"

Tina turned to pull a bubbling casserole from the oven and then grinned. "This concoction of yours smells divine. Bet we sell out before lunch is over, but don't change the subject. Something's bothering you so spill it."

I shook my head, intending to deny it but Tina just grinned and pushed me towards the empty bar. "Tina! What are you doing? I have work to do. The potatoes for Irish stew need to be chopped and we still need to – "

"It can wait. Most everything is done." She reached into the bar fridge and pulled out two cans of root beer. Popping the top, she slid one toward me and nodded. "Proceed with the explanations."

I shook my head and gave up trying to hide my feelings. Tina was relentless and besides, I did need to talk. Party girl Tina was probably not the best person to seek relationship advice from though. "I ... um, Dom just dropped me off and yelled that he loved me before he drove away."

I let out a breath. There, I'd said it out loud and it wasn't so bad after all.

Tina's eyes widened. 'You and the sexy security guy patched things up? When? How? Girl, you never tell me anything!" She took a sip of root beer. "I can't believe you've progressed this far and not told me the details." She sniffed and pretended to wipe her eyes. "Here I thought we were friends."

I laughed. "Cut it out." I sighed and decided to edit the events of last night. If I mentioned the break-in, I'd have to tell Tina everything, and right now that required expending more brainpower than I felt capable of summoning.

My conscience smote me, but I stifled it with the promise that when I knew more, I'd tell my friend the whole sordid tale of the blue diamond. For now, I'd stick with the major complication of my relationship with Dom, whatever that was.

I fortified myself with a long pull from the soda can and then told the amazed and agog Tina how Dom spent the night, carefully skipping any mention of why. "So, you see, we talked a little and ... um, did a bit more than a little and um ..." I drew lines in the condensation on the bar. "His mention of love, well that has thrown me completely off of my game."

Tina's face lit up with a smile worthy of the Cheshire cat. "Girl! Finally, you're getting a life. What's to wonder about? The guy fell for your charm and wit and is now professing undying love. From where I'm standing that's not a problem." Tina raised her eyebrow and pursed her lips. "Unless you don't return the feelings."

I gave a tight smile. Leave it to Tina to hit the ball right out of the park on the first swing. The truth was, I didn't know how I felt. He made me feel so many things- physical desire so strong it shook me and a longing for hearth and home so deep it was causing me to question my goals. I could easily see myself sharing a life and a family with him but that seemed ridiculous. We hadn't known each other for two months and besides, was a serious relationship even something I wanted right now?

I shook my head. Added to the mess with the ring ... I didn't need this uncertainty, couldn't afford the distraction from the now very real danger I faced.

I rose from the table and headed to the kitchen motioning for Tina to follow. "Honestly? I don't know how I feel. He is sweet and kind. He treats me like a rare jewel and seems to care about what I think and feel, which is more than I can say for most guys but ..."

Tina passed me and held the swinging door open. "But what?"

I walked through and grabbed an apron. "But I don't need any of this right now. I have a café to worry about." I tied the strings around my waist and picked up a knife.

With quick, efficient moves I diced two potatoes into perfect one-inch cubes and then glanced over at Tina who'd come to stand beside me. "My life is complicated, and I don't know if I have anything left to devote to a relationship, at least right now, you know?"

Tina patted me on the shoulder and then walked over to the stove, grabbing a simmering pot of meat and broth. She set the hot pan beside me and scooped up the waiting potatoes.

"I say you're thinking too much, as usual. Why not just go with it? He sounds like a great guy- who you haven't really let me meet yet I might add. Why don't you just relax and see where it goes? Don't analyze everything." She winked. "Some things you just have to let simmer, right?"

I smiled and shook my head. "Like this stew? You think I should put my relationship on low and let the flavors meld?" I laughed at Tina's emphatic nod.

"You're too much, but you might be right. I mean, no rule says I have to tell him I love him back or anything, right? I can just take it slow and see where it goes."

"Now you got it. Just go with the flow, Ivy girl, don't think so much." Tina laughed and walked off, leaving me with my thoughts. I finished chopping the potatoes and tossed them into the pot of Irish stew. A couple of bay leaves, a pinch more sea salt, and the stew was ready to simmer. I stirred it and set the flame to low, but my mind wasn't on my work.

Aside from my confusion over my relationship with Dom, I couldn't stop thinking about my godfather and the Gibbons diamond. I washed my hands and leaned against the counter, absently watching my staff hustle around the kitchen preparing for the after-parade crowd.

I was set to do a brisk business today which should have made me happy, and it would have had I been able to push aside the questions surrounding the blue diamond. Dom was convinced Jamie was involved, that he was the one responsible for all the things happening to me, but I just couldn't make myself accept that.

The paper we'd found last night was incriminating but it wasn't proof positive. Jamie had been good to me, was still good to me, and I owed him a lot. The fact that he might be involved hung over me and Dom. It put a wedge into whatever relationship we might be forging, and I didn't think we could move forward.

I shook my head and sighed. Whatever future we might have would be rough until the truth about the ring and Lorena Riordan's murder was revealed.

Dom's solution didn't sit well with me. Putting aside my concerns for our budding relationship, I didn't relish looking over my shoulder and worrying over when the next blow would fall.

I wanted answers now, wanted to feel safe again. I didn't want to live in fear for months, or maybe years, while an informant tried to ferret out information. There had to be another way.

"Hey Ivy?"

I looked up to find Tina frowning at me. "Yeah? Did you need something?"

Tina snorted. "Uh, yeah. You here on Earth would be nice. You're like a thousand miles away. I asked you three times if you want Pete to bake more soda bread."

I blinked and straightened. "We've got what, six dozen baked?" I did some quick calculations. "Better have him make another four dozen. Whatever doesn't get sold can be used for croutons."

Tina nodded. "Okay." She started to walk back to the baking area then turned and looked at me. "Something's bugging you, something other than your gorgeous guy. You got something you need to do? 'Cause, we're fine here. I brought in extra wait staff for the lunch rush and most everything is prepared."

I started to shake my head and then stopped, making a split-second decision. "You know what? I do need to take care of something. If I hurry, I can be back before the parade is over."

I untied my apron and grabbed my cell phone. "I'm gonna run over to Jamie's house for a bit. Hopefully, I can catch him before he leaves for the parade." I headed out the door. "I'll be back in a jiff."

Tina waved. "Take your time; we're fine. Better hurry though, the crowds are getting thick, and you won't make it through."

I pushed open the front door and thought Tina had never spoken truer words. People lined up five deep in front of the café and they snaked down the block as far as the eye could see.

I wriggled my way through and slipped under the rope barricade figuring it'd be quicker to walk in the street. The cathedral clock chimed. I had a little over an hour before the parade began. I dialed Dom's cell and started to jog the three blocks to the Brogan residence.

"Riordan."

I dodged a crowd of partiers and raised my voice over the noise. "Hey, Dom. I just wanted to tell you I'm on my way over to Jamie's."

"What? Ivy get back to the café; I'm heading your way. You don't need to do anything."

I skirted a group of tailgaters set up in the square. "No, I'm going to talk to him. This can't go on. I heard what you said this morning. I don't know how I feel right this second, but I do know that- "

"Ivy! You don't have to tell me anything you don't feel. It doesn't change how I feel. Look, we'll talk about it in a second. I'm threading my way through this mess of cars and ... wow! People are crazy. Ivy, just sit tight, please. We'll talk about everything just as soon as I get there."

"Dom, I'm not willing to keep looking over my shoulder and living in fear. I also can't accept that Jamie is involved. You insist he is and well ... how can we have any type of relationship with this hanging over our heads?" I paused to draw air into my lungs. "I've been thinking- "

"Stop it, Ivy! You're not thinking at all! Just go back to the café- "

"No!" I scowled at his bossy tone. "I'm going to get to the bottom of this. There is no concrete proof that he stole the ring, just suspicion. I'm going to find out what he knows and end this once and for all, so we can get on with our lives."

"No! You get back to the café and let me handle this. Brogan is dangerous. I know he's behind all of this and nothing is stopping him from-"

"He's the only one who knows what happened that night. Maybe he can tell me who is looking for the ring now. He won't hurt me, Dom. I'm just going to ask him some questions."

"Son of a bitch! You're going to get yourself killed! Just do as I say and go back to the Cosmic- "

"I'll be back in a little while. Jamie is in the parade, so I won't be long. If it makes you feel better, I'll leave my cell on. Or better yet, I'll turn on the recorder. Then we'll have everything on tape, and you'll have your proof one way or another."

I dodged a high school band milling in the street. "Look, I'm at his Square now so I'm going to hang up and switch on the recorder. I'll see you soon, and stop worrying!"

I ignored his shouted protests and hung up. I pressed the button for the record function and slipped it into my back pocket. Catching my breath, I looked around. Lafayette Square was packed with people. The side-walks were congested, and people had grills going. I smiled. Leave it to Savannahians to turn St. Pat's into a tailgater.

I wormed my way through the throng until I stood at the bottom of my godfather's steps. I hesitated. I'd told Dom Jamie wasn't guilty of anything, but niggling doubt flickered in the back of my mind.

Lorena Riordan got that ring from someone, and it got her killed, of that, I was certain. The only question that remained was from whom she took it. I climbed the steps and rang the bell, only one way to find out.

Ivy

I paced across the oriental carpet and tried to calm my nerves. Waiting for the maid to find Jaime was leaving me with way too much time to question my actions.

Now that I was standing in his library, my idea seemed foolish or foolhardy. Either way, I wished I hadn't come. Deciding to leave, I strode to the door only to stop short as Jaime entered the room, followed by a huge, mountain of a man I'd never seen before.

I gulped and planted a smile on my face. "Jamie! I was just getting ready to leave. I'm sorry to bother you. I forgot you're in the parade today." I moved closer to the door. "I'll get with you next week."

His hand clamped onto my shoulder. "Nonsense. I've always got time for you, but give me a second." He turned to the Goliath. "Go ahead and bring the car around, Vince, we won't be long."

"Sorry about that, Ivy, now then, what can I help you with?"

"Uh, Boss?"

Brogan sighed and held up a finger to me, "Sorry, Darlin', he's new." He turned to the giant hovering beside him. "What?"

"Uh, the roads are blocked." He nodded towards the windows overlooking the Square. "Can't get the car out."

Jamie's mouth tightened. "We'll leave by the alley and meet up with the parade as it crosses Taylor Street. I've notified them we'll be cutting in just before the Cathedral. Anything else?"

I tuned out their conversation but couldn't avoid staring at Jaime's driver. The man's face was covered in angry red gashes. I'd had a few of those over the years, courtesy of Sergeant.

He met my gaze and my stomach rolled. *Oh God, he knows I recognize him!*

I gulped and tried to hide my rising panic. *Oh, Dom, you were right!*

"So sorry, Ivy ...,"

I jumped as Jamie's hand fell upon my shoulder. "But as you can see, time is short today ..."

I drew a deep breath and forced my voice to remain casual as I tried to shuffle out of Jamie's grip. "Oh, I wanted to talk to you about some expansion ideas for the café, but really, it's too soon to think about such things." I stepped out from under his hand.

"Don't let me keep you. I know the parade people are sticklers for punctuality ..."

My voice quivered and Jamie frowned. "Something wrong, Ivy?" Reflexively, my gaze flitted to the driver before I forced myself to look out the window. Jamie's eyes narrowed. He looked between me and the driver a few times and then his mouth tightened.

"Vince, be so good as to shut the door when you leave. My goddaughter and I need to have a little chat."

My heart pounded in my ears and my mouth went dry. I cursed my impulsiveness, praying for divine inspiration and a glib tongue. "Seriously, Jamie, we can talk later- "

"Enough of the charade, Ivy." He sighed. "You always were too clever by half."

I shivered as he stepped closer and lifted my hand. His fingers tightened around my wrist, and I squeaked in pain. "Where is the ring?"

I licked my lips. "Wha ... what ring?" I tugged at his grip. "Jamie, you're hurting me ..."

"I know, stop playing games; I haven't the time. I know you were snooping around asking questions yesterday." He nodded towards the door Vince had just exited. "Mr. Williams can be quite chatty."

I gasped. "What did that monster do to him?"

Jamie smirked. "Why nothing, I assure you. The old man was more than willing to talk, Vince can be quite persuasive."

Tears pricked my eyes. "Jamie, what is going on? You're scaring me!"

Jamie ignored my question but released my wrist. He started to pace, his face twisted into a mask of anger and his eyes unfocused.

You just couldn't leave well enough alone. Just like your aunt. Poking your noses into things that don't concern you."

I gasped. "Aunt Fey?" I shook my head, thinking I hadn't heard clearly. "Jamie, she's dead. She has nothing to do with this."

Jamie snorted and shook his head, clearly exasperated with my ignorance. "Yes Ivy, I know she was strangled. The stupid witch tried to blackmail me." He waved his hands in the air. "Me! Who did she think she was?"

He sneered. "I searched for that ring for years. When it wasn't found on Nolan's body, it never occurred to me that she had it." He shook his head. "You know that bitch called me up and said she had proof I was guilty of fraud? Said if I stayed out of your life, she'd turn it over to me."

He waved his hands as his voice picked up volume. "On top of that, she told me I had to drop out of the Congressional race!" His lips twisted into a grotesque parody of a smile. "Said people like me weren't worthy of serving our country."

He laughed. "Didn't even ask for money, altruistic idiot!" He snorted. "I eat people like her for breakfast."

My legs wobbled. I backed away, leaning against a bookcase as I tried to make sense of what I was hearing. It couldn't be true. He was rambling. He didn't know what he was saying.

Tears streamed down my cheeks, and I angrily brushed them away. I couldn't lie to myself any longer. He knew exactly what he was saying.

He'd killed Aunt Fey. Only the killer would know she'd been strangled. The police had made it clear the cause of death wasn't released to the public.

Air, I needed air. I gagged and stumbled to the door. Throwing it open I ran into a solid wall of warm flesh. I shrieked as cruel fingers bit into my upper arms, halting my progress.

"Going somewhere, Ms. Michaels?"

I whimpered and struggled in Vince's grip, but the huge man only tightened his hold. Jamie crossed the room and grabbed my chin, forcing me to meet his eyes. "Stop fighting. You're not leaving until I say so. Now, tell me where the ring and that receipt are."

My eyes widened. I couldn't believe this was the same man I'd played countless hours of gin rummy with. He'd been my father's best friend since grade school, he'd loaned me the money to start the Cosmic Café! I whimpered. "Why are you doing this?"

"Doing what? Protecting myself from an ungrateful girl who bit the hand that fed her?" He reached behind me and flipped a switch beside the bookcase. A soft ping resonated in the room as a small door swung open.

I blinked as the opening revealed a hidden safe. Jamie punched a series of numbers into a keypad and pulled the metal door open to reveal stacks of money. He removed several thick wads and stuffed them into my front pockets.

I squirmed and tried to dodge his hands. "What are you doing? Have you lost your mind?"

An evil smile twisted Jamie's lip. "I'm doing what any decent citizen would do. Stopping a thief." He affected a forlorn look. "Imagine the public sympathy for me when it's reported that my goddaughter, the apple of my eye and pride and joy, is caught by my faithful employee in the act of stealing from me." He smirked. "It'll buy me tons of free airtime."

I gasped. "You'll never get anyone to believe that. I'll tell everyone the truth. The ring and receipt will back me up! I'll tell them how you murdered Aunt Fey- "

"Did I forget to mention the fact that you are killed while in the pursuit of your crime? Now tell me where the ring is, and I promise you won't feel a thing."

I glared at him. "Go to hell."

Jamie shrugged and nodded at Vince. "If that's the way you want to play it."

I screamed as Vince's hand connected with my cheek. My head snapped back, and the metallic taste of blood filled my mouth. Vince raised his hand to strike again, and I cringed as I waited for the blow.

The door to the library burst open to reveal Dom and a terrified maid. Vince clamped his hand over my mouth and pulled me out of sight of the door.

"Where's Ivy, you bastard!"

"What the- "

I squirmed and clawed at the meaty hand preventing me from shouting. "I'm sorry, Mr. Brogan." The maid stammered. "I told him you were busy, but he pushed right past me."

Jamie waved her away. "It's all right, Maria, Mr. Riordan is expected."

Vince wrapped his free hand around my neck and propelled me forward as he crept toward the door.

"Sir? The parade committee has called three times. They say you're late. Should I ..."

Jamie nodded. "If they call again, tell them we had car trouble but we're on our way."

The door clicked shut and Vince shoved me toward the couch, launching himself at Dom. Fists clenched, Dom swung at Jamie. I yelled but my warning came too late.

Vince's fist collided with Dom's face with a sickening crunch, sending him to his knees. Vince hauled him up and pinned his arms behind his back.

I ran forward but Jamie grabbed my arm. Furious, I swung at him. He slapped me and pushed me back to the couch. "If you know what's good for you, girl, you'll stay there."

Jamie smoothed his suit coat and turned to face Dom. "Now then, Mr. Riordan, how nice of you to join us. Perhaps you can convince your girlfriend to tell me where my property is."

Dom spat at him. "Go to hell."

Jamie clucked his tongue. "My, my ... so many people seem to wish my departure."

Dom glared at him and then looked at me. "Are you all right?"

"She's fine, Mr. Riordan, for now. Tell me where my ring is and both of you might remain that way."

Dom snorted. "Like I believe that. You have no intention of letting us live, any more than you did my mother."

"And Aunt Fey!" I nodded as Dom's eyes widened. "He killed her Dom. He said she was strangled and that wasn't-"

"Yes, yes, Ivy. You're becoming redundant." Jamie crossed the room to stand in front of Dom. "As for your mother? She was a whore ... and a thief."

Dom struggled against Vince's hold, his eyes were wild and full of hate. "My mother was no whore, and you are the thief."

Jamie smirked. "Really? Can one steal one's own property? A matter for philosophers, I think." He shrugged. "Regardless, your mother found the ring and stole it before the courier arrived. Had the stupid maid not let her in here, the ring would've been safely on its way across the Atlantic to reside in the vault of a private collector. Who knows, she might be with you today."

He screwed his face into a mockery of sadness. "Alas, she too thought to blackmail me." He snorted. "As if I'd ever leave my wife for a common trollop available to the highest bidder."

"My mother could have done better than a thug like you!"

Jamie punched Dom in the stomach. "Really, Mr. Riordan. I'm just a typical businessman."

Dom gasped and slumped in Vince's grasp. "You're typical ... typical politician anyway." He panted for breath. "Fit right in with the Washington crowd."

Jamie smiled. "Believe me, Mr. Riordan, I intend to."

"You won't get away with this, Brogan. The cops are on their way as we speak."

"But Mr. Riordan, we won't be here." Smirking, he crossed to the couch and hauled me to my feet. "Now then, we should be off; the parade is waiting."

"Where are you taking her?"

Jamie ignored Dom and dragged me towards the door. I met Dom's gaze. He stared at me then looked down and kicked with his foot. I frowned but he made the same motions again and I caught on. I nodded and licked my lips, ready to act.

"Brogan! I have your ring!"

Jamie jerked to a stop and swung around, and I made my move. I clawed Jamie's arm and stomped on his foot. Jamie let me loose and I turned in time to see Dom swing at Vince.

He clipped the man's jaw and then lashed out with his foot. Vince dodged the kick and slammed his fist into Dom's jaw.

I screamed as Dom was thrown back by the force of the blow. My stomach heaved as his head connected with the bookcase and he slumped to the floor.

"Oh my God, Dom!" I ran to his side and cradled his head in my arms, feeling for a pulse. *Thank God, he was still breathing.* I used my shirt tale to wipe at the blood trickling down his cheek. *What had I gotten us into?*

"I'm so sorry, Dom. So, so sorry ..." I sniffed and leaned down to kiss his forehead when rough hands hauled me to my feet.

I kicked at Vince, squirming and trying to claw at his face. "You bastard!"

Vince waved me away like an annoying cloud of sand gnats. "You want me to get rid of them, boss?"

Jamie shook his head. "No, I'm afraid Mr. Riordan's arrival calls for a change in plans. Put that money back, Vince." He tossed me a box of tissues and walked to the mirror, straightening his tie. "Clean yourself up, Ivy. You get to ride in the parade."

I blinked. "What?" I rubbed my sore arms as Vince released me. "I'm not going anywhere with you."

Jamie made no comment, simply looked at Vince and then back at me. Dom grunted as Vince's foot connected with his ribs.

"Stop!"

"Going to freshen up then?"

Vince pulled the money from my pockets and shoved me toward the mirror before joining Jamie at the desk.

I swayed and gripped the sides of the console table for support. I looked like death warmed over. My lip was swollen, and dried blood crusted one corner of my mouth. I swiped a tissue over my cracked lip, but nothing could hide the bright red hand imprint on my cheek.

I sniffed and fought tears. What were we going to do? A glance at Dom showed he was still more unconscious than not. His legs were moving restlessly but his eyes were closed. I doubted he'd be of any help.

I closed my eyes and prayed for a miracle. Dom had said he'd called the police, but even if that were true, they'd never make it through the throngs of people clogging the streets.

I needed to think. With Dom incapacitated, it was up to me to get us out of the mess I'd made. I leaned forward to examine the split in my lip and a series of beeps sounded from my pocket. I smiled.

Watching the two men from the mirror, I pulled out my cell phone. The red light in the upper right corner showed the recorder was still rolling.

At last, a miracle. I set the phone down on the console table and arranged a handful of tissues to shield it from view, but I needn't have bothered. Both men were occupied. I tuned in to what they were saying and then gasped.

"Ms. Michaels will ride with me in the parade. Her good behavior will be assured by the knowledge that you have her boyfriend stuffed into the trunk. When the parade is over, Ms. Michaels can tell me where the ring is."

Vince nodded. "And if she don't tell you?"

"Why then, perhaps I'll let you seek your revenge on that beast she calls a cat."

An evil smile spread across Vince's ugly face. I shivered and hoped the police found my phone.

Rain on My Parade

Dom

I blinked and strained to see in the darkness that surrounded me. My head throbbed and a dull ache plagued my lower back. I stretched and then groaned as pins and needles raced through my legs. Gritting my teeth, I forced myself to sit up and then wished I hadn't as knife-like pain shot through my already aching head.

"God! What the ..." I raised my hands above my head, feeling the ridges of the hard metal object blocking my way.

I lay back and tried to clear the cobwebs from my foggy brain long enough to figure out where I was. I stretched out one leg and found I couldn't extend it the entire length, the same thing for my arms.

Panic crept in, making my heart pound. Where the hell was I? My mouth went dry; the space was so tight and dark that it felt like a coffin.

I drew several deep breaths and strained to regain command of my senses. I closed my eyes and concentrated. Without the panic and pain clogging my brain, I became aware of several things.

First and most importantly, I was moving, slowly, but it was movement, and my nose was assailed by the smell of car exhaust.

Then there were the sounds. Laughter, music, car horns, and noisemakers- I was near the parade route.

Oh hell! I'm in it. The bastards had locked me in the car trunk. They were probably sitting in the front right now. Brogan would be smiling and waving at the crowds while he plotted my and Ivy's demise.

A chill went through me. What had they done with Ivy? I had to get out. I mustered every ounce of strength I had and kicked at the truck's lid. Nothing. Sucker didn't budge so much as an inch.

I thought about yelling, but with the crowd and the marching bands, there was no way anyone would hear. All I'd manage to do was use up precious oxygen.

I felt all around, twisting my body to expose more of the floor. There was bound to be something I could use to open the lid. Everybody had junk in their trunk, didn't they?

Cursing my luck for being kidnapped by a neat freak, I'd all but given up when my fingers bumped against something cold and metal. Relief poured through me. I felt my way along the length of the item and realized it was a tire iron.

My luck was turning. Now, if only I could maneuver the thing and get leverage. I wrestled the iron out from under the carpet, managing to bang my chin in the process. Finally, I got the flat end wedged against the trunk's lock.

Ivy

I wriggled and squirmed in an effort to relieve the numbness in my butt. Perching on the backseat of a convertible was not conducive to comfort. Jamie sent me a warning glare before plastering a phony smile back on his face. I rolled my eyes. The way he waved to the crowd you'd have thought he was the Queen of England.

I watched the Irish dancers leaping and frolicking in front of their car and gritted my teeth. Everything felt surreal. Crowds of screaming people dressed in green, bass drums and tubas booming in my ears, and a maniacal killer pressed against my side.

I jerked my head around as a loud thump echoed from the trunk. Dom! God, I hoped he could breathe. At least he was moving; surely, that was a good sign. My lip trembled. He'd looked so pale and lifeless when Vince had dumped him into the trunk. I'd been sure he was dead or soon to be.

I closed my eyes and swallowed past the lump in my throat. All of this was my fault. If I hadn't been so stubborn and stupid, I'd be dishing out Irish Stew and Soda bread back at the Cosmic and Dom would be anywhere other than inside Jamie's trunk.

I looked away and hoped Jamie was unaware of Dom's efforts. I forced myself to smile and wave as I focused on a plan. Vince was driving the car, but I'd seen the bulge under his jacket. Easy enough to throw the car into park and jump out, but would he do that with a crowd of onlookers?

I didn't think so. I could jump out and get lost in the crowd before he could reach me but what about Dom? I couldn't, and wouldn't, leave him at the mercy of Jamie and the hulking Vince.

Another thump followed by a muffled curse drew my and Jamie's attention. Dom was definitely awake, and from the sounds of it, he was trying to open the trunk.

Fingernails ground into my forearm, making me wince. "Eyes forward please, and pretty smiles for the crowd. Your boyfriend will never manage to free himself."

I glared at Jamie and jerked my arm away. My skin crawled at his touch. I searched his handsome face for some sign of the man I'd thought I knew but all I could see was the monster who'd killed my aunt.

Tears welled and flowed down my cheeks as I realized Aunt Fey had given her life to protect me. All those years when I wouldn't visit, wouldn't even talk to her-I wished with all of my heart I could see Aunt Fey just once more to tell the woman how much I loved her.

As grateful to my aunt as I was, I couldn't help but wonder why she hadn't just taken the ring and the receipt to the police. Had she done that years ago none of this would be happening. I scrubbed at my eyes and wiped the tears from my face; thanks to the evil man beside me, I would never know my aunt's reasons.

From the corner of my eye, I saw the trunk lid bounce. Hope flared to life. Jamie underestimated Dom. I drew a deep breath and made my decision. If Dom could open the trunk, I'd make a run for it and pray Vince followed me, leaving Dom to get help.

Aware of Jamie's eyes on me, I turned to my left and smiled at the crowd. I waved and threw a handful of candy to some excited children, trying to act normal and ease his suspicions.

The wheels were turning in my brain. My plan seemed too simple but sometimes the simplest things worked, if only Dom could get free.

My mouth went dry, and a lump formed in my throat as I saw the trunk lid bouncing. I casually slid my legs closer to the side of the car and tensed, preparing to run.

A fine sheen of sweat formed on my brow as the seconds ticked by with no noise coming from the rear of the car.

I held my breath and hoped Dom hadn't passed out, or worse. I exhaled and let my shoulders droop, convinced my planning was for naught.

The trunk lid sprang open, making me jump. People in the crowd started yelling and pointing. Jamie yelled at Vince to stop the car as he made a grab for my arm, but I dodged his hand and swung my legs over the side.

My feet hit the pavement as the car jolted to a stop. I ran to the back of the car and helped a struggling Dom sit up. My eyes widened as the car door slammed and Jamie shouted for Vince to hurry.

"Dom! I'll get Vince to follow me. You get help."

"Don't be a fool, help me out- "

"He's coming, just get away from here. It's me they want."

"Vince! Don't let her get away!"

Jamie's shout startled me into action. I dropped Dom's hand and ran towards the crowds lining the street. Like a chain reaction, the parade participants were coming to a standstill behind the stopped car.

Horns started honking. The road was filling with hordes of confused and angry people. In minutes, Jamie's car would be surrounded.

I moved to the back of the sidewalk and turned. Standing on tiptoe, I could just see Dom limping through the crowd. Hopefully, he would do as I'd said. I glanced at the car and saw Jamie standing in the backseat. His hand shaded his eyes as he scanned the sides of the road. I ducked, but too late. He pointed in my direction and then yelled something.

Vince nodded and took off across the road, shoving people out of his way. I gulped and started some shoving of my own. My plan was working but Vince was meaner than I'd thought. His disregard for everyone in his way would soon put him right next to me.

"Excuse me ... please! Let me through ..." I shoved and twisted through the masses of bodies, frustrated with my lack of progress. Fear hammered inside me.

I glanced back to see him wading through the throng. My stomach lurched when I realized his size made his task much easier.

The crowd thinned as I made it to the corner. I stepped out into the road and wove my way through a group of stalled marching band members to make it to the Square. I stopped to see where Vince was. His bulky frame towered over most people. The crowds slowed him down, but he was catching up.

I had to keep moving, but where? I drew a deep breath and got my bearings. A block ahead I could see a mounted policeman. I felt a glimmer of hope. If only I could make it before Vince caught me.

I looked back to see him stuck amidst a group of drunk and rowdy college kids. *That should buy me a little time.* I turned to run just as three pops followed by piercing screams rang out from behind me. My heart skipped a beat as someone yelled, "Lookout! He's got a gun!"

I looked over my shoulder to see the crowd parting and Vince barreling towards me. Oh, God! In a fair race, I'd never beat him. I searched for a place to hide, and my gaze lit on an alley. Perfect.

I took off, dodging people, grills, and dogs. I ducked down the alley and slid behind a dumpster, hoping Vince hadn't seen me.

The strong scent of urine and rotting garbage burned my nose and maggots crawled up the side of the box. I held my breath and watched the alley's entrance, hoping to see Vince run by.

Minutes passed with no sign of him. Panicked screams, mingled with sirens gave me hope that Vince was soon to be in custody. My legs trembled with exhaustion and a Charlie horse was forming in my calf.

Seeing no sign of my pursuer, I risked a stretch. I leaned against the brick wall of the building behind me and extended my leg, sending a beer bottle rolling across the cobblestones just as Vince came into view.

Dom

I groaned and pressed a hand to my aching ribs. Every step I took brought a fresh wave of pain, but I pressed on, determined to keep Vince in my sights. The woman needed a keeper.

What was she thinking? I'd never leave her alone to deal with Brogan's thug. I shoved another drunken reveler out of my path and spotted Vince's hulking shape wending through a marching band. Farther on, I saw Ivy flit through the Square. Where was she going? She needed to run toward the crowd, not away from it!

I groaned again and broke into a trot. When I caught up to her, I'd beat her for sure, or kiss her senseless for scaring me so badly. Sirens wailed, drawing nearer, giving me the strength to pick up speed.

I crossed the Square a hundred yards behind Vince. A few more minutes and I'd catch him; of course, what I'd do then was anyone's guess. I ran around a group of teenagers mocking the parade and headed up a side street.

Up ahead, I saw Vince dart into an alley. The sirens were louder now. Any minute, they'd arrive and start searching for the crazy guy wielding a gun. I just needed to find Ivy and keep her safe. The police would do the rest.

I slowed as Vince neared the alley's entrance. If memory served, the alley wasn't a dead-end so I wouldn't be trapped. Then again, I couldn't trap Vince, either. What was the guy doing in there and where was Ivy?

I backed up flush with a building and risked a quick peek around the corner. My heart skipped a beat. Ivy was cowering against a dumpster, looking down the barrel of Vince's gun.

Time seemed to slow. I crept around the corner, keeping my eyes on Vince's hand as I picked my way down the debris-littered alley. So far, I'd managed to stay out of Vince's line of sight, but Ivy's wide eyes and gaping mouth showed she was well aware of my presence.

I raised a finger to my lips and took a cautious step. I was picking my way around a heating unit when I heard Vince cock his gun. My stomach rolled. I needed a distraction. "Vince!"

The big man swung around. Our gazes locked. A foul grin lit his face as he raised his gun.

"Ivy, run!" I ducked behind the heat pump. An explosive pop reverberated in the small space as searing pain flared in my upper arm. Blood was flowing down my arm.

God! Had I been shot? My heart pounded in my chest and bile rose in my throat. I ignored it, rising to a crouch and peering down the alley. Relief flooded through me as I saw Ivy round the far corner. Thank God, she'd finally listened to me.

I sank back behind the heater and looked at my wound. There was a lot of blood, but a quick and painful probe didn't reveal any hole. It seemed the bullet had grazed me, but the beating I'd endured was catching up to me. My ribs ached and my head felt like it might explode at any minute.

The crunch of gravel alerted me to Vince's presence. I shook off the dizziness threatening to engulf me and crawled along the wall, behind the heat pump. Vince's shadow fell across the wall where I'd been. I kept inching forward. If I could get behind Vince and take him by surprise, I just might have a chance.

"Come out, come out wherever you are."

I sneered at the big man's taunts but remained quiet. A few more feet and I'd be in position.

"Boss says I get a taste of that fine piece of tail before I off her. Too bad you'll already be dead; I would've liked to make you watch."

My jaw clenched and my teeth ground together to stay quiet. God, I was going to enjoy taking the asshole down. I reached the end of the unit and paused, listening for Vince.

"Yer bleeding like a stuck pig. Not gonna last long. Come out and I'll go easy on ya."

The dumb oaf wasn't even trying to hide his position. I raised my head to see Vince bent over at the other end of the heating unit. I drew a deep breath and pounced.

Breath whooshed from my lungs as I collided with Vince's broad back and clung to him, pummeling him with my good arm. Vince grunted and stood up, shaking me off as easily as a duck would water.

I groaned as I landed on my injured arm. I used my legs to scoot along the cobblestones as Vince loomed over me, gun in hand. The irony of the situation struck me. In all of my years as a cop, I'd never pulled my weapon or faced one down.

"Whatcha gonna do now?" The thug pulled the hammer back, the click abnormally loud in the quiet alley.

I gulped and prepared to meet my maker, but then my eyes widened, and my throat tightened. Standing directly behind Vince was Ivy, holding a pitifully small piece of pipe.

I tensed and rolled as Ivy swung at Vince's head. Vince squeezed off a shot that narrowly missed my head and then whirled in Ivy's direction.

I staggered to my feet and launched myself at Vince, catching him around the thighs. We fell to the ground and rolled, coming to rest in a tangled heap at Ivy's feet. Vince struggled to rise and made a grab for Ivy's leg.

I pushed myself to my feet and planted a sharp kick to Vince's side. Vince got to his feet and swung around, wildly waving the gun as he tried to get his bearings.

"Damn it, Ivy! I told you to run."

"I'm running now!"

I ducked under Vince's outstretched arm and grabbed him around the middle in a bear hug. Fueled by anger and adrenaline, I pummeled Vince again and again.

Vince grunted and swayed on his feet. I seized my chance and kicked him in the knee. We both went down. Vince slammed his fist into my stomach, making me see stars.

I shook off the pain and made a grab for the gun. We rolled across the dirty ground. Vince brought his arm in close to his body and pulled the hammer back. I rolled to the side and used every ounce of strength I had to force the big man's hand back.

One loud pop and both of us went limp. I shoved Vince's crushing weight off of me and closed my eyes. I gulped for air and pressed my hand to my throbbing side. I struggled to rise but the effort was too much. The last thing I heard was the wail of sirens mingled with Ivy's screams.

Three Little Words

Ivy

I huddled beside the EMT and prayed. They kept assuring me Dom was breathing but he was so pale and still. There was so much blood. It covered his chest and arms and crusted in his hair. I bit back a sob and stepped back so they could move Dom to the stretcher.

I glanced over to Vince's lifeless form. Blood oozed from the hole in his chest, forming a pool at my feet. I backed away and tried to convince myself to pity the dead man. It was a hard sell.

"Ma'am, is your name Ivy?"

I tore my gaze away and focused on the young woman in front of me. "Yes." I cleared my throat. "Yes, I'm Ivy."

The woman nodded. "Okay. We were getting ready to take Mr. Riordan to the hospital but he's awake and asking for you. He's refusing treatment."

"What?" I rushed toward the ambulance doors. My eyes widened as I saw Dom sitting up. His legs were dangling from the side of the stretcher while he supervised a paramedic wrapping his ribs and securing a bandage on his arm. "What are you doing? Lie down!"

Dom shook his head and beckoned me closer. The medic shook his head and walked away as I drew alongside the stretcher. Dom's arm snaked out and pulled my head down. "Are you insane-"

His lips claimed mine in a fierce kiss, cutting off my words. I pulled back afraid of causing him more injury, but his hand held mine fast while he increased the pressure on my mouth.

With a whimper, I sagged against him in relief. A kiss like that surely meant he was okay. I carefully wound my arms around his neck and returned the kiss, putting every bit of love I felt into it.

Dom tore his mouth from mine and drew a ragged breath. He rested his forehead against mine and fought for breath. "Don't ..." he gulped more air. "Don't you ever do something that stupid again."

I leaned back to meet his eyes. "What-"

"You could have been killed. The next time I tell you to run, you run like a bat out of hell!"

I rolled my eyes. "Are you seriously scolding me for saving your butt?" I tried to push him down onto the stretcher, but he resisted, grabbing my hand and kissing it.

"I wouldn't have needed saving if you'd listened to me in the first place and stayed in your kitchen."

Guilt roared through me. He was right. He'd been right all along, and my stupidity had almost gotten both of us killed. Tears filled my eyes. I stroked his cheek, careful of the rapidly swelling knot on his jaw.

"Oh Dom, I'm so sorry." I hiccupped. "Can you ever forgive me? How can I ever make it up to you?"

Dom brushed the tears off my cheeks and dropped a light kiss onto my parted lips. "Quiet ... there's nothing to forgive." He waved my concern away and slid to his feet. "And stop fussing, the bullet just grazed me. Give me a tetanus shot and some pain pills and I'll be fine. My ribs are the worst of it. Medic says I need x-rays to be sure, but they don't feel broken."

I raised an eyebrow. "Dom, you are covered in blood and were unconscious. You need a hospital."

He shook his head and then swayed.

I wrapped an arm around his waist, careful to avoid his bandaged ribs. "See?"

Dom grunted and started walking toward a waiting police car. "I didn't say I wasn't hurt, just don't need a hospital. Most of this blood is Vince's but he did beat the crap out of me." He took several more halting steps. "I'll do much better with your careful ministrations and tender mercies than what any nurse could give me. Consider it your penance for this mess."

My mouth dropped open and then I laughed. "You are too much."

They continued across the road and joined the cluster of policemen. Dom leaned against the cop car as men milled around greeting him and cracking jokes. I smiled as Detective Hallowell's friendly face broke through the crowd.

"Hey Dom, glad to see you on your feet. Thought for sure you were a goner."

Dom laughed. "Can't get rid of me that easily, Paul."

The big man laughed. "Nah, you've taken worse. Hey, you remember the time we chased that perp through Forsyth Park, and you tripped over a dog and went flying across the sidewalk?" He chuckled. "Man, you were a mess! And what about that tangle with the pimp over on 35th_ "

"All right, Paul! We get the picture."

A chorus of laughter rang out and then the uniforms waved and returned to the crime scene.

Detective Hallowell nodded towards me. "Ms. Michaels, I read your statement. You're a lucky girl."

I looked at Dom and smiled. "Yes, I certainly am."

Dom squeezed my hand. "Paul, can I give you a statement tomorrow?"

"Sure, sure Dom. We're about ready to make the collar. That guy is some piece of work. We followed your tip and showed up at his house, but the maid said he was in the parade. Found Ms. Michaels' cell phone before we headed to the parade route. That is some crazy stuff! How'd a guy like that … imagine if he'd won the election!" Hallowell shook his head.

"You should have seen the chaos on Bull Street! When we got there, Brogan was standing in the back seat yelling and cursing. The crowd was so thick around the car; everyone hollering at him, and the Parade Marshall was fit to be tied.

We hauled Brogan out of there, but the chief wouldn't let us arrest him. He's at his house until the D.A. gives the word but I'm bettin' it'll happen sometime today no matter what Brogan's high-priced lawyer says."

"Man, this town's gonna go nuts when the trial starts! I'm thinking we got an airtight case with the confession. It's his voice, and the stuff Ms. Michaels' aunt had squirreled away will be icing on the cake." He laughed and smiled.

"That cell phone was some good thinkin' little lady. Hope it'll be admissible in court, but that's for the D.A. to worry about." He shrugged and motioned towards the car. "I'll get with ya tomorrow afternoon on that statement, Dom. Since you ain't going to the hospital, you want a ride home?"

"That'd be great." Dom nudged me into the backseat and slid in beside me. "Take us to Ivy's place over on Gwinnet, would ya?"

Dom leaned back and closed his eyes as the car pulled away from the curb. A thousand questions ran through my mind, but I held my tongue. His face was white, and his lips were pinched. I hadn't missed his wince when they got into the car, either. I contented myself with holding his hand. Time enough for answers when he was well. The important thing was he would recover. I shuddered as an image of Vince's blood-drenched corpse rose in my mind.

Minutes later, Detective Hallowell helped Dom up the stairs and left with the promise of a phone call tomorrow. I bolted the door and set the alarm then helped Dom to the bathroom. "I still think you should just get into bed."

Dom snorted and tried to get his shirt off. "I'm covered in blood and alley crud. There's no way I'm not showering; here, give me a hand, will ya?"

I helped him remove his clothes and the bandage around his ribs. I turned on the shower and adjusted the temperature. "You want me to help you, or can you manage?"

Dom stepped under the spray and grinned. "I can manage but it'd be a more interesting experience with you in here."

I laughed and pulled the curtain closed. "You are banged up and bruised all over, that should be the farthest thing from your mind. I still say you should be in the hospital."

"I'm sore and I've got a killer headache, but I'd rather be here with you so quit nagging. You sound like a wife."

I stilled. "You say that like it's a bad thing."

Dom peeked around the curtain. "Just a joke, doll, just a joke."

I forced my lips into a smile. I was unsure just how his 'joke' made me feel. Everything was happening so fast. It seemed unreal that just this morning I'd been wading through the mystery of the blue diamond and my feelings for Dom. Jamie's imminent arrest put an end to my immediate problem but Dom's close call with death only deepened my confused feelings concerning their relationship. My head was spinning and added to that was the realization Aunt Fey had died trying to protect me. Emotions swamped me. I needed to think.

I grabbed a towel from the cupboard and hung it beside the shower. "Dom, if you can manage here, I should call Tina and make sure the café is running smoothly. I'll also get us something to eat."

Dom turned off the water and stepped from the shower. "I'll be fine but I'm not hungry. I sure could use some coffee though."

I bit my lip. "Would hot cocoa do? Or I could run to the café for some coffee."

Dom grabbed my hand and pulled me flush against him. "Cocoa is fine. You will not leave my sight." He dropped a hard kiss onto my lips. "Got it?"

I grinned. "Yes sir! I'll obey orders from now on, I promise."

Dom pushed me towards the door and reached for the towel. "Don't make promises you can't possibly keep, my love."

I grinned and hurried to the kitchen. I shook my head. Dom was being very free with the "L" word, and I still didn't know exactly how I felt. *Could he really love me? Do I love him?*

We'd known each other such a short time and most of that had been spent fighting each other or bad guys. With a return to normal life, would they find they had nothing in common?

I bit my lip to keep it from trembling. I didn't have any answers, wasn't even sure of my own feelings. I knew one thing, though; Dominic Riordan was an important part of my world, and I wasn't ready to lose him. Might never be ready.

I sighed. There was so much to think about and process. I made a quick call to the café. Tina's breezy assurance that the cash register looked like a leprechaun had lost his pot of gold made me smile. I hung up the phone and stepped over Sergeant to grab a saucepan from the drain rack. I rinsed the pan with cold water to keep the milk from sticking and then poured in a generous amount of almond milk. Adjusting the burner to low, I added a drop of vanilla, more vanilla in the form of flavored sugar, and a cinnamon stick. As it started to warm, I added several heaping tablespoons of dark cocoa. I stirred the creamy concoction and pushed aside my tangled feelings; time enough to sort them out. Dom wasn't rushing me.

For now, I needed to come to terms with my godfather's villainy. I'd trusted him, thought of him as a father. His betrayal of that trust, along with his willingness to cause me harm, pierced my heart.

I swallowed hard and replayed Jamie's insane rant. He'd shown no remorse for anything he'd done, not even killing my aunt. Nothing mattered to him but securing his rise to power. Anyone who got in his way was expendable.

I poured the steaming liquid into two large mugs and added a dollop of whipped cream and a sprinkle of nutmeg. Questions rolled around in my mind. So many things I didn't understand.

How did Aunt Fey even get the blue diamond in the first place and why, if she'd known what it was, didn't she take it to the police? I sighed; with Aunt Fey dead I'd never know.

"Ivy? You get lost?"

I smiled and set the hot mugs onto a tray. "Nope! I'll be right there. You just get into that bed and stay there!"

"Yes ma'am. Ordered to bed by a beautiful woman, every man's fantasy!"

I laughed, grabbed a handful of Tina's oh-so-yummy gingersnaps, and clicked off the light.

I entered the room to find Dom propped against the pillows watching the news. I handed him a mug and climbed into bed, mesmerized by the events unfolding on the screen.

A beautiful blonde newscaster stood in Lafayette Square reporting on the bizarre events that had disrupted the Saint Patrick's Day parade and led to the anticipated arrest of Congressional candidate and local businessman James Brogan. The camera zoomed in on his front door as it swung open to reveal a cluster of uniformed officers leading a handcuffed Jamie through a perp walk.

Light bulbs flashed and reporters shouted questions as the stone-faced man was frog marched down the steps and shoved into a waiting car. The scene changed to the reporter as the car pulled away from the curb.

"A press conference is scheduled for nine this evening, but we can tell you the basic facts. Following a tip from an unidentified man, police raided Mr. Brogan's home. Finding evidence, they as yet haven't specified, they proceeded to the stalled parade route and removed Mr. Brogan from the scene. Police aren't commenting on the parade disruption involving Mr. Brogan's car or the identity of the man and woman seen fleeing the scene."

"At this time, it is not confirmed if or how the body of an unidentified man found in an alley just off of Bull Street ties into this case. We'll keep you posted as developments unfold; for now, this is Connie Lee, reporting for Action Ten news."

Dom clicked off the television and turned to me, raising his mug in silent salute. My smile was wobbly. "Well, I guess that's that, then. I never thought we'd live to see it through."

Dom snorted. "It was by the grace of God, love, trust me. A couple more punches and I would've had it." He set his drink down and pulled me close to his side. "You wouldn't have had to put up with me ever again."

"I don't mind putting up with you."

He kissed the top of my head. "That's good to know since I don't plan on going anywhere any time soon."

I smiled. He was such a good guy. A true-blue kind of man that would stick by me, through thick and thin. My heart said to take a chance and confess the love I was feeling but my mind said caution. Too many years of living with Aunt Fey and her *friends* had left their marks and I didn't trust my judgment.

Look how wrong I'd been about James Brogan. I sighed. Why, oh why had my aunt chosen to live such a lifestyle? Had she any idea what it did to a kid's mind?

"Ivy? What's wrong?"

I shook my head and avoided his eyes. "Nothing. I was just thinking about everything that's happened today. I can't believe Jamie killed my aunt and I really can't understand why she tried to blackmail him." I sniffed. "I can't help but wonder why she never went to the police. I mean, if she had, we would have lived here in Savannah and had a normal life."

"Ivy, look at me."

I wiped a bit of moisture from the corner of my eye and turned to look at Dom. His gentle smile warmed me but also made me want to cry in earnest. I was full of such baggage where men were concerned. Could they ever have a life together?

Dom cupped my chin and stroked my cheek. "Look, Ivy, you need to let all of this go. Your aunt had her reasons. I guess you'll have to trust that they were good ones because we'll never know what motivated her." He sighed and dropped his hand.

"Hell! I could say the same about my mother. If I hadn't been obsessed with having a place in society, I'd still be alive. Honestly? I guess I'm comforted by the fact that if your aunt and my mom hadn't done what they did, we'd have never met. That's a thought I'd rather not entertain, ya know?"

I smiled and squeezed his hand. I looked into his eyes and saw nothing but love blazing there. Perhaps his outlook was the right one to take.

"I guess you're right, but it just seems a terrible waste." I turned my head and my gaze lit on the spiral-bound sketchbook laying on my nightstand. I leaned over and pulled it onto my lap.

"Look at these. I found them when Tina and I cleaned out Aunt Fey's apartment." I thumbed through the first couple of pages as Dom leaned over my shoulder. "She was so talented. Had she stayed in one place and concentrated on her art, who knows what success she may have found."

Dom reached out and took the book, examining the finely drawn charcoal renderings of me and Savannah's various attractions. "She was good, really good. Her likeness of you is uncanny."

He flipped through the book until he reached blank pages. "Must be like looking in a mirror." He was handing the book back to me when something floated out from between the pages and landed in my lap. "What's that?"

I picked up the paper and slowly unfolded it. "I don't know. It must have been stuck in the back; I never looked farther than the last sketch." I scanned the paper and tried to stop my heart from racing. "Dom! This is Aunt Fey's handwriting. I'd recognize her chicken scratch anywhere."

"What's it say?"

"I don't know ... it's addressed to me." I bit my lip and started reading. Tears flowed down my cheeks as I finished. With a trembling hand, I tucked the note back into the sketchpad and turned to Dom.

"Aunt Fey ..." I cleared my throat and brushed the tears from my eyes. "Aunt Fey must have realized how dangerous her blackmail idea was. She wrote to me in case something happened to her ... oh Dom! If I'd just searched that notebook a little harder, none of this would have happened. She explained everything-told me about the ring and that sales slip- God! Why didn't I look?"

"Ivy, you couldn't have known, so quit beating yourself up. What else did she say?"

"Ummm ..." I lowered my eyes, unsure of how to tell him what I'd read. How would he react upon hearing of my aunt's involvement with Lorena's death? Would he feel so disgusted by Aunt Fey's actions that he wouldn't want to be with me?

The confession had startled and upset me, and it wasn't even my mother; I drew a deep breath. Whatever happened, I had to tell Dom. He deserved closure too.

"Ivy? Whatever it is ... just tell me."

I nodded and braced myself for his reaction. "It seems Aunt Fey knew about your mom's murder or at least suspected it." I felt Dom stiffen and rushed on. "It says she was with her boyfriend, Frank Nolan, that night and sat in the car. She thought he was going to make a drug deal- they were dealing."

I swallowed past a lump in my throat. "Anyway, she just thought he was meeting someone at the Waving Girl Statue to sell some pot, but she heard a loud pop like gunfire. When he got in the car, he had blood on him and smelled smoky. She knew something bad had happened, but when she asked, he just slapped her, tossed a small box into her lap, and told her to put it somewhere safe."

I looked over at Dom and cringed. His face was white and a muscle in his jaw twitched. I gulped and tried to explain my aunt's actions. "Dom, she says she didn't make the connection to your mom's murder until she read it in the paper, and by then, Frank Nolan was dead. Some rough-looking guys came around asking questions. Then the cops started in and well, she was scared.

She opened the box and the diamond reminded her of the big robbery. She didn't know what was going on, but she was afraid for her life."

My heart sank as I laid my hand on his arm and felt him flinch. He said he loved me, but would he turn from me now because of what Aunt Fey had done?

I swallowed hard. "Dom, please try to understand. I know what my aunt did was awful. If she'd called an ambulance that night, your mom might not have died, or if she'd gone to the police, you wouldn't have had to suffer from not knowing all these years."

I bit my lip, wondering what Dom was thinking. He kept his eyes lowered but his body was rigid. There was nothing I could do but tell him everything and let the chips fall.

I sniffed. "She begs me to forgive her for being a coward. She says it wasn't any excuse, but she was afraid of Nolan. He beat her, then when he died, his friends started harassing her. She'd been arrested for possession once so her experience with cops made her afraid to go to them. When she suspected Jamie's involvement, well, she just hid the diamond and ran."

My shoulders drooped. Dom sat rigidly beside me not making a sound. I braced myself and waited for his rejection. Surely, knowing my aunt had been party to his mom's murder would change his feelings for me.

I couldn't blame him, but my heart still ached at the thought of him leaving.

After several minutes of silence, Dom let out an explosive breath and pulled me into his arms. I gulped and tried not to get my hopes up. He seemed to be all right with what I'd told him, but my mind screamed for a definite answer. I cleared my throat. "Dom? Are you okay with all of this? I mean, I'll understand if you want to leave."

"What?" He squeezed me so tight I squeaked. "Why would I want to leave? You're not making any sense." I wriggled from his arms and turned to look at him.

The look in his eyes encouraged me. All I could see was confusion, no sign of anger or disgust. "I ... well, I thought you might be ... that you might not want to be with me after what my aunt did. I mean, I wouldn't–"

"Ivy, stop." He shook his head. "Why would something your aunt did or didn't do, affect how I feel about you? They aren't related at all. Sure, I would've liked to know who killed my mom long ago. As far as saving her ... she was shot through the heart, Ivy. No one, or nothing, would have saved her life."

He shrugged. "I'm shocked to find out what your aunt knew but that has no bearing on us." He squeezed my hand. "I love you and I'm not going anywhere. I'm happy everything has come full circle. Now we both have answers to our pasts which means we can look to our future." He leaned down and kissed me. "And I do mean *our* future."

I gulped and tried to keep my lip from trembling. My heart thudded in my chest. He really did love me. I felt it and saw it in his eyes. But what did he see in our future? Was this a casual thing or were we headed for deep territory? Unsure just what Dom's vision of our future entailed had me running scared, yet another trait I shared with my aunt.

I drew a deep breath and tried to push aside the tangled emotions coursing through me. I told myself to be content with today, to stop fretting about what might or might not be. My heart refused to listen. I needed to know if he was interested in something more than a casual fling.

Years of watching my aunt flit through one man after another had left its mark. I couldn't give my heart away without assurances I was loved just as deeply and that a man was just as committed as me. But what right did I have to ask Dom for that? I'd almost gotten him killed!

"Ivy?"

I blinked as Dom waved a hand in front of my face.

"Snap out of it; you're a million miles away and by the look on your face, I'd say you were trying to solve the problems of the universe."

A puzzled and slightly worried frown marred his handsome face. A hesitant smile curved his lips. "What's wrong?"

I forced myself to smile. "Nothing! It's nothing." I started to pull away. "I should let you sleep."

Dom grabbed my hand and tugged, pulling me off balance. I tumbled across his chest. "Dom! You're ribs!"

He shrugged. "Pain killers are kicking in, s'no big deal. Now tell me what's wrong. You've got a funny look on your face, and you're tense."

"Don't be silly."

"Ivy, don't play games, okay? We've been through too much for that, don't you think?"

I sighed and nodded. He was right. Whatever else, there should be honesty between us. "I ... um, I was going to wait until you felt better to discuss it."

Dom rolled his eyes. "Out with it."

I swallowed hard and searched for words. "Well, it's just ... I was wondering where we go from here."

Dom frowned. "Go? Why do we have to go anywhere? I'm content to lay here beside you for a good long while."

I huffed. "That's just it. I guess I'm wondering how long a while is to you?"

I watched as realization dawned in Dom's eyes. I bit my lip and looked at him from beneath my lashes. *God, I felt like a fool- a desperate, clingy, needy fool.* Why couldn't I have kept my mouth shut?

"Ivy, are we talking about our relationship here?"

I nodded; afraid my voice would crack if I spoke. To my relief, Dom smiled and pulled me closer. With our mouths inches apart, he whispered. "I love you."

Tears formed in my eyes and flowed down my cheeks. I swallowed hard and forced the words past the knot in my throat. "I love you, too."

He cupped my chin and brushed the tears away. "Then what's the problem?"

I sniffed and brushed a strand of hair from my face. "I ... I guess I'm wondering what's next. I mean we haven't known each other very long. We've only had one date!" I scooted off the bed, gesticulating as I gathered steam. "I mean, this is crazy. People don't just meet and fall in love! It takes time, years maybe! And what about- "

"Ivy stop!" Dom's shoulders shook as he held his ribs and laughed. "Girl, you are too much. If it's dating you want, I'll take you on one every night! I'll even buy you candy, send you flowers, the whole nine yards. I can't argue with your logic; everything you've said is true. All I can say is you occupy my every thought."

He crooked his finger and then patted the space beside him. I bit my lip but joined him back on the bed. He smiled and grabbed my hand. "The week you wouldn't see me was a nightmare. Everywhere I went I was re-minded of you. A tie-dyed shirt, a big white cat ... hell, even the grocery store!"

I laughed. "The grocery store?"

Dom kissed the tip of my nose. "Yes, I was staring at the almond milk like a lovesick schoolboy; it was disgusting." He cuddled closer and nuzzled my neck. "All I know is I can't imagine spending a day without you, okay? Can you trust me enough to welcome me into your life?"

I sighed and nodded. I'd heard the ring of truth in his voice, saw it in his eyes. He loved me and wanted to be with me. I could accept that and build on it. It was a start.

The bed dipped as Sergeant landed at the foot. The big blue-eyed monster stalked across the covers, inching his way up the mattress. My eyes widened when I saw what he carried in his mouth. I eased from Dom's side and muttered for him to stay still.

Dom stiffened. "Why? Is that thing going to attack me?"

I shook my head and stifled a laugh. "Just watch."

Sergeant reached Dom's side, leaned over, and dropped a ratty toy mouse onto his chest, then planted himself in Dom's lap and proceeded to bathe.

Dom's mouth dropped open. "What's he doing?"

I laughed and snuggled against his side. "Welcoming you."

The End

Thank you for reading Ring of Lies,

I hope you enjoyed meeting Ivy, Dom, Tina, & Sergeant Pepper; if so I'd appreciate a review.

Ready for the next adventure of the Cosmic Café Crew?
Dive into Tina's story in
Broken Chords, Available July 22nd

Excerpt: Broken Chords

Prologue

Instrument cases and amplifiers stacked to the ceiling divided the room into narrow aisles. A single bulb in the hallway barely penetrated the gloom, casting the space into pockets of light and shadow.

Outside, the wind whistled and howled, and rain battered the hull, muting all sound. At the beginning of one aisle, a drum kit was partially unpacked. Symbols and drumsticks sat next to a keyboard stand; the snare and kickdrum were still encased in their canvas shrouds. Two guitar stands and a foot pedal board sat nearby.

Farther into the room lay a body, sprawled amidst colorful bits of wood, lengths of wire, and steel strings. A pool of blood was forming under his head, creeping across the floor as the ship pitched and rolled with the storm. A torn piece of paper was clutched in his hand.

A shout disturbed the silence, followed by the slam of a metal door.

Tina

Four more steps. That's all it'd take to get me through the door. I took two of them and then chickened out and reversed course for the third time. I gave myself a mental shake and an order to suck it up, Buttercup: I had to go in, no choice.

I snorted. Well, no real choice. If I didn't reconcile with my father then my best friend and nominal boss, Ivy Michaels, would not let me buy into her café, and to be a full partner in the Cosmic Café I'd meet the devil himself; an aging rock legend should be a piece of cake in that competition.

It'd been over ten years since I'd willingly been in the same room with my dad. I hadn't been able to avoid him at my mother's funeral, but even then, our conversation had been minimal. After that, the only way I'd seen him was on the cover of tabloids.

I'd been happy to see he'd gotten sober, but that change wasn't enough to lure me back into a relationship and I was fine with that; despite the opinions of Ivy and the shrink she'd made me visit.

I huffed. What neither of them seemed to understand was that my father's sobriety or lack thereof was not the main reason I'd cut ties with him. My avoidance of my dad centered around the company he kept; specifically, the predator known as Richard Warner.

My stomach heaved at the thought of the man. Up until now, I hadn't thought-The invitation had been last minute, and Ivy had pushed me to accept it before I could talk myself out of it.

Last minute shopping, packing, and getting coverage for my shifts at the Cosmic Café ... only now, with the ship making its way out of the harbor, was it hitting me that Warner was probably on the cruise; all my life, where ever my dad went, Warner was never far behind. Why would this be any different?

I swallowed hard and backed away from the lounge doors. How would I avoid him? My hands began to shake ... I couldn't do this!

I paced the hallway and contemplated alternatives, but I knew there weren't any, not really. If I didn't buy into the café, Ivy would have to find another investor because the loan she'd gotten from her godfather had been called in. I cursed James Brogan and his legal troubles for starting all of this!

Of course, ranting at fate wasn't going to help. What I needed was Dutch courage, just a shot or two of bourbon-heck, I'd settle for a glass of Pinot to calm my nerves, but my drinking was what had gotten me into the current mess ... I rolled my eyes, just thinking about Ivy and the whole Christmas disaster.

I mean, so we'd been suspected of murdering the neighbor. We'd solved the case, and everything was fine.

I didn't know why Ivy was in such a snit almost three months later-

"Ma'am, this is a restricted area at this time, can I help you?"

I jumped and spun around to find a giant of a guy frowning at me. He wasn't dressed in the ship's officer uniform; those white shirts and shorts combo cracked me up, but even in his sport coat and chinos I could tell he was official, he had law enforcement written all over him. I gulped and pinned a smile to my face. "Uh, hey how ya doin?"

He smiled, but it didn't reach his eyes. "Ma'am. This area requires a pass." Crap, I'll bet he was talking about the lanyard that was sent with the cruise tickets ... I dug in my bag, but I was pretty sure it was sitting on the dresser in my cabin. Double crap ... I met his eyes and tried to look cute.

My gaze skittered away because he wasn't buying it. I noticed his name tag, Tyson Penshaw, Chief of Security. I shook my head. Just my luck to run into Dudley Do-right.

"Uh, it's uh, I didn't realize that I needed, and it didn't go with this dress so-"

"Ma'am," he placed his hand at my elbow and started to nudge me towards the atrium. "You'll need a pass -"

"Kristina?" Chief Dudley and I both turned to see a tall woman with short, spiky orange hair striding toward us.

She held a clipboard and was dressed in leather pants and a white t-shirt; gotta be with my dad's band, though I couldn't place her.

"It is Kristina Crawford, right?" She smiled and offered her hand. "I'm Nikki Hardy, Assistant Road Manager for Eclipse." She pointed at my dress. "Love the outfit!"

Oooh, I didn't know her, but she'd admired my lime green mini dress and vintage white go-go boots and seemed intent on rescuing me ... I'd take it.

"Thanks, Chief, I'll take it from here."

Dudley dropped my elbow but didn't back off. "She doesn't have a pass, all entry to band areas are restricted to pass holders-"

"I know, I set up that policy." She smiled but it was one of those firm, no-nonsense, back-off kinda smiles; I was really liking her now.

The security chief scowled. "If you compromise once-"

"Normally, I'd agree with you, Mr. Penshaw, but you know Chad Crawford, lead singer for the rock band Eclipse? The band you're trying to protect?"

The security chief nodded.

"Well, this is his daughter, whom he hasn't seen in ages and is anxiously awaiting the arrival of so if you don't mind, we'll just make an exception this once," it was her turn to guide me by the elbow, "have a great day,

Chief, come along Ms. Crawford, we'll get you another lanyard."

Giving a little wave to the chief, I matched my steps to Nikki Hardy's and then slowed as I realized she was leading me through the Alchemy Lounge doors I'd been trying to avoid when this whole mess started- crap, out of the frying pan and all that ...

"Uh, so ..." I stopped on the threshold of the door she was holding open. "Uh, so how long have you been with Eclipse? It's pretty cool, you being the road man-"

"Go on, Kristina, he won't bite."

Okay, she'd seen right through me, maybe I needed to revise that liking her thing.

I fidgeted with the hem of my dress then realized I was probably flashing someone and smoothed the fabric back in place, not that it covered much more than the tops of my thighs; oh fudge, why had I worn it? I stood out like a sore-

"Hey, take a deep breath."

I blinked and met her gaze. Her eyes were a vivid aquamarine, probably colored contacts, and they were radiating warmth and concern which was nice but also a bit weird; it was like she knew me. "Have we met before?"

I bit my lip. That had come out a bit more blunt and sharp than I'd intended, even for me.

She smiled and shook her head. "No, but your dad and I are friends" she shrugged. "He talks about you a lot." She took my hand and gave it a slight squeeze. "Just relax, no pressure, breath in, that's it, now let it out, all the negative energy is flowing out with that breath, you are lighter ..."

Her voice was soft, really gentle like a warm breeze. I kept eye contact with her and found myself doing just what she said. In and then out ... "Wow, how did you do that?" I shook my head and smiled. "I feel ... well ..." I shrugged.

"Lighter?" Nikki laughed and gave my hand a final squeeze. "It's nothing, just a bit of relaxation technique. In my line of work that skill comes in handy."

I frowned and then it clicked. "Oh, you mean stage fright?" I snorted when she nodded. "Chad Crawford has never been afraid of the spotlight in his life! He owns whatever stage he's on."

Nikki laughed. "Oh yes, no argument there." She tipped her head toward the front of the lounge where a group of men were talking; my dad included. "Chad doesn't have stage fright, but we all have our moments, and Cliff is a bit neurotic."

I laughed because the bass player for Eclipse was just what she'd said, my mom had always said he was high-strung. I grinned at Nikki and let her nudge me into resuming the trek toward my dad. "I won't tell him you said that."

She grinned. "He wouldn't deny it!" She kept me chatting until we were within earshot of my dad. "Chad? Look who's here!"

My heart kinda rose in my throat as my dad turned and rushed toward us.

"Kristina Carol! You came-"

His arms were wide, and I cringed, knowing he was gonna hug me. I'd missed him, I could admit that, but I wasn't quite ready for warm and fuzzy. I stepped back and nodded. "Uh, I go by Tina now, Chad."

The smile dropped from his face. "Uh, of course, I shoulda known." He glanced at Nikki then lowered his arms, shoving his hands into the front pockets of his ridiculously tight jeans.

"How could you?"

He sighed and looked at the far wall. His jaw was set, and a nerve ticked in his cheek. I could all but hear his teeth grinding. I was regretting my tone, it'd upset him and now we stood in awkward silence; oh yeah, this was gonna be the cruise from hell, and worse, I had to do it sober.

Nikki cleared her throat. "So, is this your first cruise?"

I took back the not liking her thing. "Uh, it's my first rock and roll themed cruise but my best friend, Ivy, and I did four days to the Bahamas."

Nikki's eyes widened. "Nice, the Bahamas are awesome, aren't they Chad?" He grunted something as Nikki plowed on, bless her heart. "The Firestorm Tour did two nights there last year."

I nodded but the chit-chat went in one ear and out the other. I was busy watching my dad. He kept glancing at Nikki, and she'd give him this little head nod, kind of encouraging him or something; it was weird and familiar in a motherly ..., no! It made me think of a long-married couple kind of thing; Nikki knew my dad far better than in a road manager way.

Huh, wasn't sure how I felt about that. Nikki Hardy was probably ten years older than me? Maybe a little more. If I had to guess, she was forty, forty-one ish.

I did some mental math. Not cradle robbing exactly and he certainly didn't look his age. I snorted. Chad Crawford wasn't gonna disappoint his legion of female fans any time soon. He still had the long hair, golden brown to match his perpetual tan, barely any lines around his mossy green eyes, and his penchant for painted-on faded blue jeans and form-fitting t-shirts proved his devotion to clean living ... hey, that was probably a safe topic.

I waited until Nikki ran out of breath. "So, Chad," he flinched, and I guessed it was because I was using his first name. I felt bad about that too, but I was only able to take one step at a time; meeting at all was the first one. "You're looking good, keepin' the groupies happy."

Nikki laughed and my dad's lips twitched for a minute before he joined in. "Smart mouth. It's dedication to exercise and clean living."

I nodded. "So, it wasn't just a passing fad ..." His sobriety was just as notorious as his addictions; the car wreck that had killed Kev Lerner, Eclipse's drummer, had sent shock waves through the music scene. A tragedy all around, but the fact that Chad had been driving fueled the media frenzy to unbearable heights.

I had already cut ties with him by that point, but it was impossible not to hear about it on every TV station and magazine cover. The speculation had been that he'd be charged with vehicular manslaughter, but surprisingly, my dad had been legally sober at the time and the wreck was blamed on weather conditions; it'd been snowing heavily, an infrequent event even in the Georgia mountains.

His eyes clouded a bit, but he gave a half-hearted smile. "Nope, going on ten years clean, made it past fifty."

I snorted. "Uh, past fifty-four old man, you'll hit the big five-five this year."

He mock-shuddered. "Why ya gotta remind me, kid"

I smirked. "You fishin' for compliments?"

He snorted and shook his head. "Nah, jokes about age are just that; doesn't bother me to hit another birthday."

He raised his eyebrows and cocked his head to the side. "Better than the alternative, don't ya think?"

What I thought was gonna remain a mystery because a commotion at the back of the room drew our attention. "Ah, what now?" Chad made a disgusted sound and threw up his hands and Nikki started cursing under her breath.

I followed their gazes and gasped as my nightmare came true; Richard Warner was on the ship. My fingers curled into fists as a rock formed in my gut. Could this cruise get any worse?

Warner was drunk, high, or both. He ambled across the stage, getting in the way of the techs and roadies trying to set up. I searched for an excuse to leave and prayed he'd stay on the other side of the room.

"Nikki, I thought you'd-"

"I tried, Chad! I personally escorted him to his cabin, but he wasn't happy about being on the lower deck."

Nikki rolled her eyes and began telling my dad how Warner had pitched a fit after finding out he wasn't staying on the private floors like the band members.

My father snorted. "What more does he want? It's a free vacation for him and it isn't like anyone expects him to actually work!" He snarled. "I still don't understand why Rob included him."

My eyes widened. Never before had my dad taken that tone or even uttered an impatient word about Warner; maybe there was trouble in paradise? One could hope-

"You idiot! I'm gonna break your neck if -"

A crash on the stage, followed by curses and threats drew my gaze back towards the stage in time to see a guy about my age with his hands around Warner's throat.

Two roadies and Benny T, the new drummer for Eclipse were righting the equipment that Richard had knocked over but, in a testament to Warner's popularity or lack thereof, no one seemed in any hurry to pull the angry guy off of Warner.

Nikki huffed. "I better break that up. That kid has murder in his eyes."

My dad snorted. "If the fool had knocked over my bass, I'd look like that too!"

Nikki laughed and was about to walk over when one of the roadies stepped in and shoved Warner down the stage steps.

Nikki and my dad sighed in relief but my heart started pounding because Warner now had my dad in his sights. He was stumbling his way across the room, all the while griping to my dad.

I caught a few slurred complaints about his room but most of what he was ramblin' about was unclear and I didn't care. I just wanted far away from him.

I started to back away, no matter what Ivy or the shrink she'd made me talk to had to say, I was not dealing with my father and the walking waste of oxygen he called a personal assistant.

Chad turned and gave me an anxious look. "You're not leaving? We're almost done setting up. I thought we could have dinner before the meet and greet-"

"Well, lookee here! It's my baby girl ..."

My mouth went dry as the drunken fool closed in on me. I spun around and rushed to the exit, ignoring my dad's calls to wait. My hands connected with the door lever.

Feeling like the hounds of hell were nipping my heels, I rushed through the door and straight into a wall of warm muscle.

"Ooomph,"

"Whoa, where's the fire?"

I tried to stop, but momentum was not my friend and my sudden reverse didn't suit my high-heeled boots. My ankle twisted as one boot lost its heel.

My savior clasped my upper arms, steadying me as I leaned over, unzipping my vintage treasures. "Crap, they're ruined!" I slid them off and looked up. The thanks died on my lips. "Ian?"

"Tina?"

I closed my eyes and gulped. Really, what gods had I ticked off? Not only did I get close quarters with my estranged father, but the universe had seen fit to put my biggest fear and loathing in the form of Ricky Warner into the mix and now, now I got to run into my ex, who I had never wanted to be an ex, lover.

I forced a smile I was far from feeling. "Ian, um, what a surprise!"

A lopsided grin stretched across his handsome face. "Surprise is an understatement." He shook his head, "What are the odds?"

I snorted. The way my luck was running, I wouldn't even hazard a guess. Wishing the deck would split apart and devour me, I tried for casual and uninterested. "So, yeah, incredible, running into you, literally!"

He smiled, flashing the dimple that I adored. "How long has it been? A year, year and a half?"

Two years, four months, six days, and a handful of hours ... but who was counting?

My hands started to shake. I couldn't do this. The shock of the slime ball Warner and now Ian ... I forced words past the lump that was starting to clog my throat. "Uh yeah ... look, it was nice seeing you again, but I've got to-"

"Ian, are you not going to introduce me?

My gaze flew to the short brunette with bright red stiletto nails clinging to Ian's arm like a limpet. My eyebrows rose. Oh yes? Did I also get an ex-lover's girlfriend? Why yes, it appeared that I was to have that privilege. How did that saying about karma go?

"Uh ...Tina this is, uh ..."

The woman huffed and nudged Ian aside as she thrust her hand towards me. "I'm Doctor Judith Fogarty, Ian's fianceé, and you are?"

Her words slammed into me like a sledgehammer. My stomach rolled and my heart started pounding again; I didn't need this! My face felt hot, and I fidgeted under the woman's stare. "Uh, I'm uh ..." I forced my brain to function even though most of it was in shock. "Tina, um Tina Crawford."

I glanced at Ian. He was staring at his fianceé. I frowned; Ian's mouth was hanging open as if he was shocked, and he was glaring at her. I heard him say something to her then he turned to me and flashed a tense smile. "Uh, we aren't, there's been no discussion about getting married."

The doctor huffed and glared at Ian. I shook my head, whatever was going on with Ian and his whatever she was, it was no concern of mine. That ship had sailed regardless of my heart's continued ache... I bit my lip and tried to force down the tears that were threatening to fall.

Too many emotions, too many old memories, and too many tangled cords of broken relationships were tugging at me and all I wanted to do was escape; To curl into a fetal position, preferably with a bottle of bourbon, and block out the whole terrible, no good, very bad day.

I stammered congratulations and turned, rushing toward a flight of steps that led somewhere; didn't matter, anywhere was better than where I was.

"Tina!"

Ian's hand closed around my arm. I paused on the second step and closed my eyes, begging for some kind of divine assistance because if I didn't get out of there I was going to lose complete control of my emotions. I tugged and Ian released my arm. I half turned but avoided his eyes. "I've got to go Ian, but it uh, it was nice seeing you." I set my bare foot on the next step. "Enjoy your cruise!"

He huffed. "Wait, please!"

The please got me. I turned and met his eyes for an instant before lowering my gaze to study the multicolored swirls on the carpet.

"Thanks, I won't keep you." He nodded back towards the lounge. "I gotta get in there, my band is playing this cruise, but maybe we could get together later? Drinks? Or Dinner?"

Small favors. A gig meant he'd be busy for a good portion of the nine days at sea. I glanced at him. "Uh, we'll see. I'm here with my dad and we haven't seen each other in about ten years so ..."

Ian's eyebrows rose. "Wow, I uh, you never mentioned your father when we were ... I mean," he shrugged.

"Guess I thought he was dead. But that's great you two are getting together, bring him to a show, I'd love to meet him."

I smiled and started back up the steps. "We'll see. He's actually working on this cruise too, so our time together will be limited." I pointed towards the Alchemy Lounge and told a little white lie. "Think we're getting an early dinner before he has to be back in there ..."

Ian frowned. "Your dad works for the cruise line? Or is he with one of the bands? What's his name, maybe I know him!"

"My dad is Chad Crawford. I'll see ya around, Ian." I raced up the steps, ignoring his shocked questions.

I fell into the first empty deck chair I found and leaned over with my head between my knees. I wasn't hyperventilating, but it was a near miss.

God! Why had I told Ian who my dad was? It came out before I had really thought about it because all I could concentrate on was Ian had a fiancée and Richard Warner was on-board, and how the hell was I going to make it through the next week without a drink?

But Ian was like a dog with a bone, and he would surely worry me to death until I explained how we'd dated for over a year and I had failed to mention my connection to one of his all-time favorite bands.

This was ridiculous; I needed a drink! Ivy and that shrink were unreasonable, no one could be expected to absorb the kind of emotional body blows I'd suffered in the last couple of hours without support.

I was weak, I freely admitted it, but one drink wouldn't hurt, and Ivy would never know.

I scooped up my ruined boots and made a beeline for the Tiki bar.

Broken Chords
Available July 22, 2022

Also By Rachel Lynne

Holly Jolly Jabbed
A Christmas novella set in the Cosmic Café Universe
When someone gets their tinsel in a tangle ... the holly isn't so jolly!

It's Holly Days on Parkview Place and all of the businesses in the Parkview Merchant Association are decorated for the season, and the weekend tour groups they all count on to plump up their bottom lines.

But not everyone is happy with the association or its plans and when the Association Chair is found jabbed in the neck with the vintage finial formerly atop the Cosmic Café Christmas tree, chefs Tina and Ivy are the prime suspects.

The police are convinced they have an open and shut case, so the ladies are grilling their neighbors and sifting through clues, but stirring up the past could cook their goose.

Fey Goes to Jail

Meet Ivy's crazy Aunt Fey in a prequel available only to my newsletter subscribers!

Fey Michaels, a cashier at an Oklahoma Indian Casino, lives by the motto, don't retrace the footsteps of your past, you might fall in.

She lives and loves freely, making the most of her one bite at the apple called life, but being the sole guardian for her ten-year-old niece, Ivy, isn't always conducive to being a free spirit.

Knowing a child needs stability, Fey tries to settle and keep her feet on the ground, but hooking up with a Shaman, who thinks ten is the perfect age to begin exploring his personal brand of spiritualism, sets off a chain of events that puts Fey in the crosshairs of law enforcement and Ivy in mortal danger.

Fey and Ivy will have to think fast and keep their cool if they want to make it off of the Reservation alive.

www.rachellynneauthor.com

Made in the USA
Columbia, SC
02 December 2024

47270992R00152